DESCENT

HILLAR FILE : 4991.09

By R.A. Howes

Descent : Hillar File : 4991.09

Renee Anne Howes

Where is BaaBaa?

A TIDE OF THE STARS CODEX

DESCENT

HILLAR FILE : 4991.09

RA HOWES

VENGEANCE
PUBLISHING

2024 REVISED EDITION

*In the spirit of reconciliation, the author acknowledges the Traditional
Custodians of country throughout Australia and their connections to land, sea
and community. They pay their respect to their Elders past and present and
extend that respect to all Aboriginal and Torres Strait Islander peoples today.*

First Published in 2022, ISBN: 9780645061512
by Vengeance Publishing

PO Box 34
Mickleham, Victoria, Australia, 3076

Second edition published 2024, ISBN: 978-0-6457603-2-3

by Vengeance Publishing

Email info@vengeancepublishing.com.au for any queries regarding
this work or special order requests.

Edited by: Pen to Print Australia

Cover art and layout by Vengeance Publishing.

Artwork/Elements sourced from Pixabay, Fiverr, Creative Market
and created by Vengeance Publishing. Vengeance Publishing has done
its best to only source and use art/elements made by real Terrans.

A copy of this edition has been registered with The National Library
of Australia and the State Library Victoria.

**TO MY FAMILY
ALWAYS CHASE THE STARS**

TERRAN STANDARD CALENDER

8 hours = 1 standard

24 hours or 3 standards = 1 rotation

7 rotations = 1 sequence

4 sequences or 28 rotations = 1 cycle

13 cycles = 1 revolution

DATE FORMAT

Revolution : Cycle : Rotation

ABBREVIATIONS

TCE : The Confederate Era

AUTHOR'S NOTE FOR THE 2024 EDITION

I will never be satisfied with this book. Born from a need to define Eric as a character, I am still not confident that I have accurately portrayed him. A family man, honest and hardworking, Eric has seen the worst a society obsessed with power and control can do. Despite everything done around and to him, he remains at his core a good man. So, knowing that, the question was, what could Hawke and The Brethren offer him to make the life of a pirate worth it?

As Tolkien once wrote in his foreword to the 1966 edition of *The Lord of the Rings*, 'The most critical reader of all, myself, now finds many defects, minor and major, but being fortunately under no obligation either to review the book or to write it again, he will pass over these in silence, except one that has been noted by others: the book is too short.'

I have not rewritten or added to this content but have refreshed, corrected some terms and, hopefully, made this a little clearer. And, at least for now, it is time to let Eric have his adventure and the pages to make his choice.

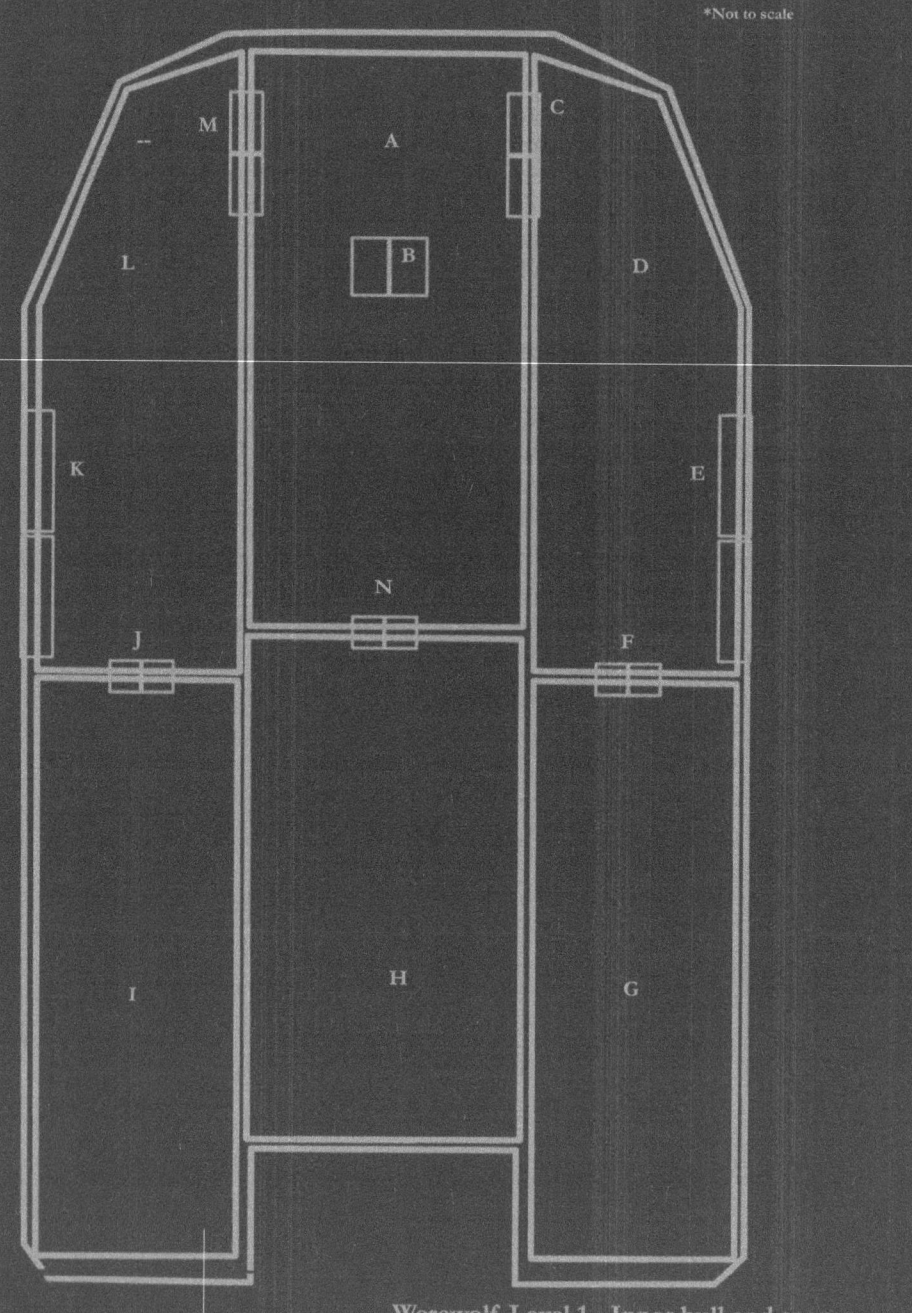

A- Cargobay 1
B- Cargobay 1 Floor Airlock
C- Cargobay 1 to 2 Airlock
D- Cargobay 2
E- Exterior Cargobay 2 Airlock
F- Cargobay 2 to Engine 2 Airlock
G- Engine 2
H- Hangar

I- Engine 3
J- Cargobay 3 to Engine 3 Airlock
K- Exterior Cargobay 3 Airlock
L- Cargobay 3
M- Cargobay 1 to 3 Airlock
N- Cargobay 1 to Hanger Airlock

*Not to scale

Werewolf Level 1 - Inner hull and rooms

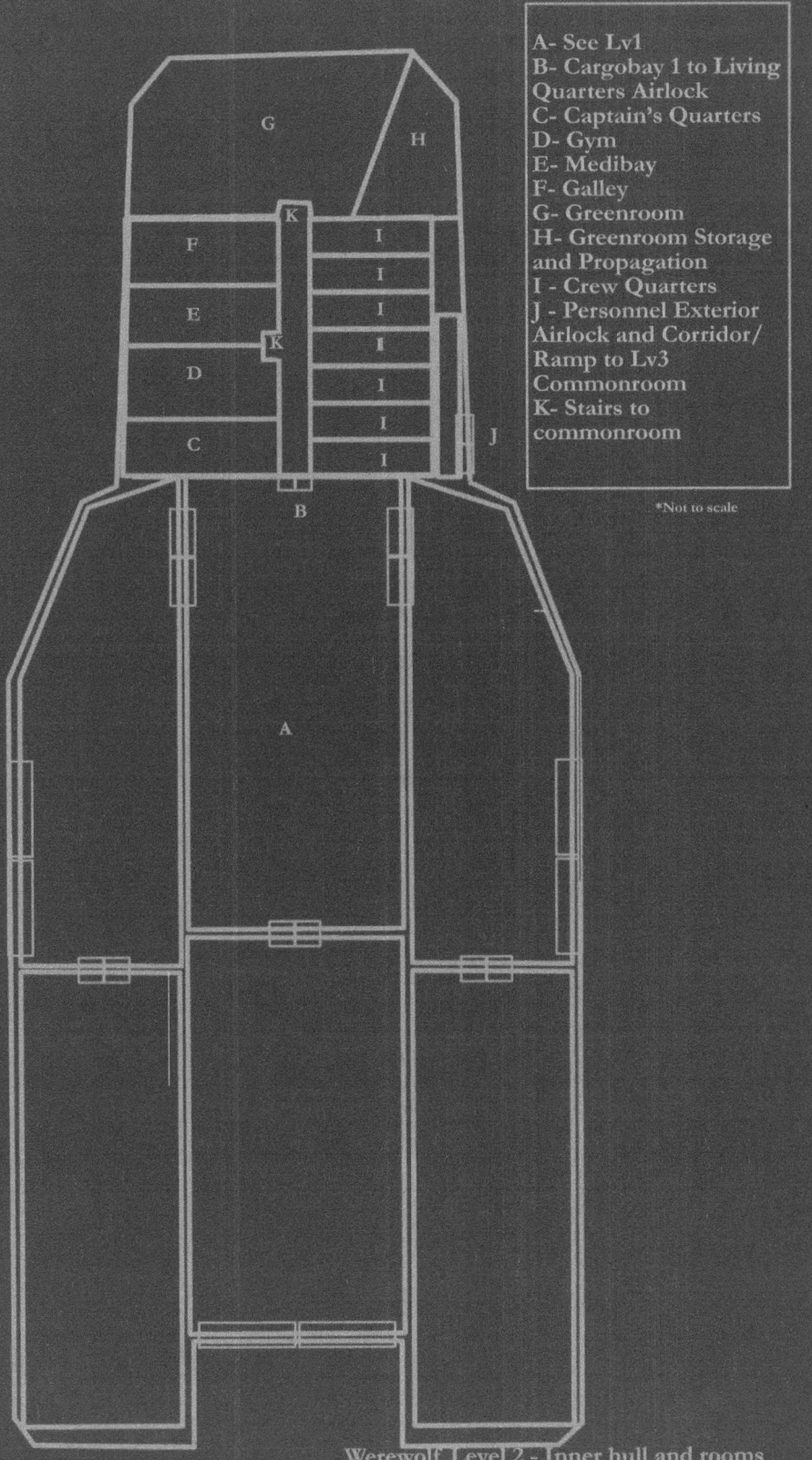

A- See Lv1
B- Cargobay 1 to Living Quarters Airlock
C- Captain's Quarters
D- Gym
E- Medibay
F- Galley
G- Greenroom
H- Greenroom Storage and Propagation
I - Crew Quarters
J - Personnel Exterior Airlock and Corridor/Ramp to Lv3 Commonroom
K- Stairs to commonroom

*Not to scale

Werewolf Level 2 - Inner hull and rooms

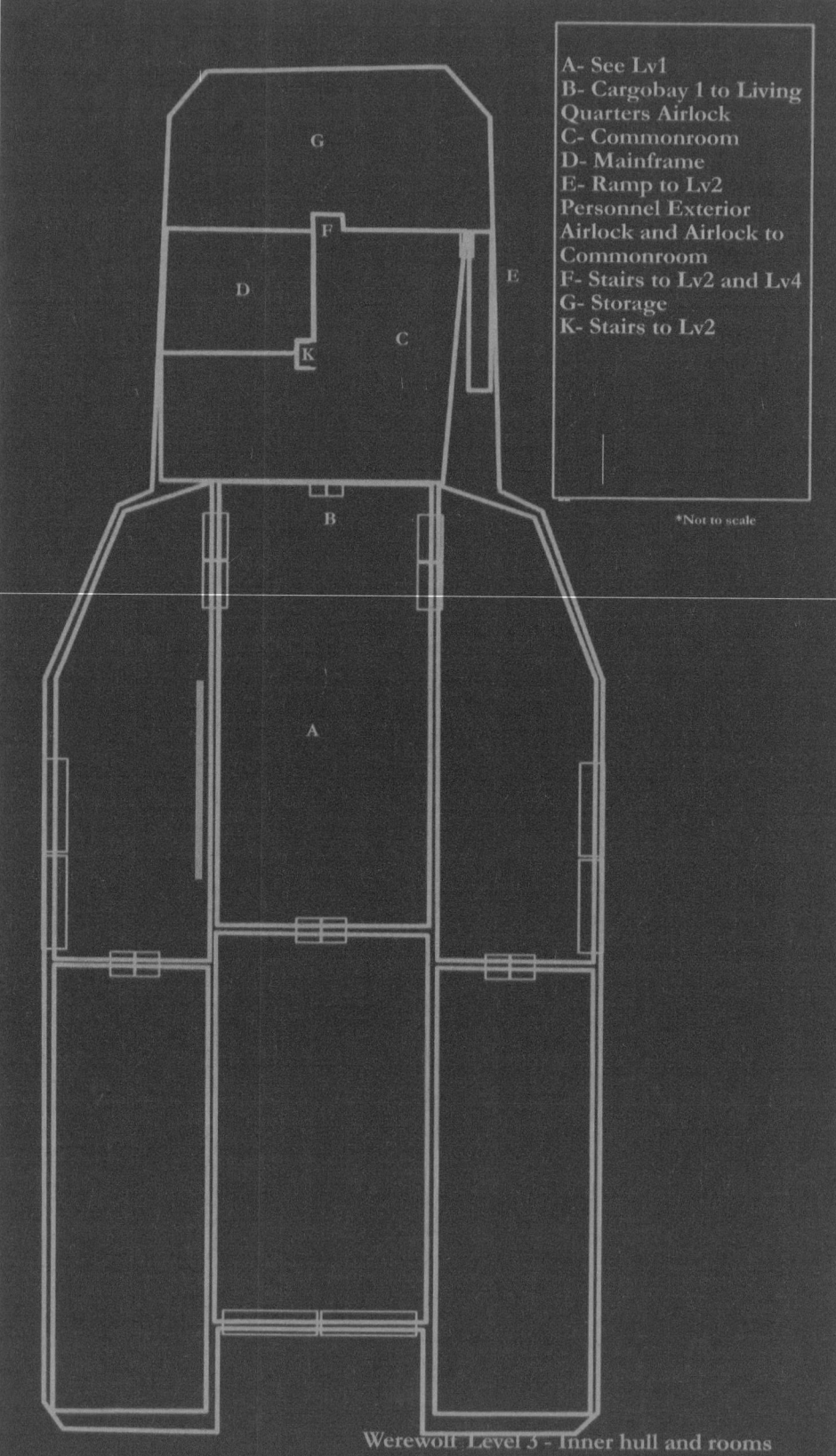

A- See Lv1
B- Cargobay 1 to Living Quarters Airlock
C- Commonroom
D- Mainframe
E- Ramp to Lv2 Personnel Exterior Airlock and Airlock to Commonroom
F- Stairs to Lv2 and Lv4
G- Storage
K- Stairs to Lv2

*Not to scale

Werewolf Level 3 - Inner hull and rooms

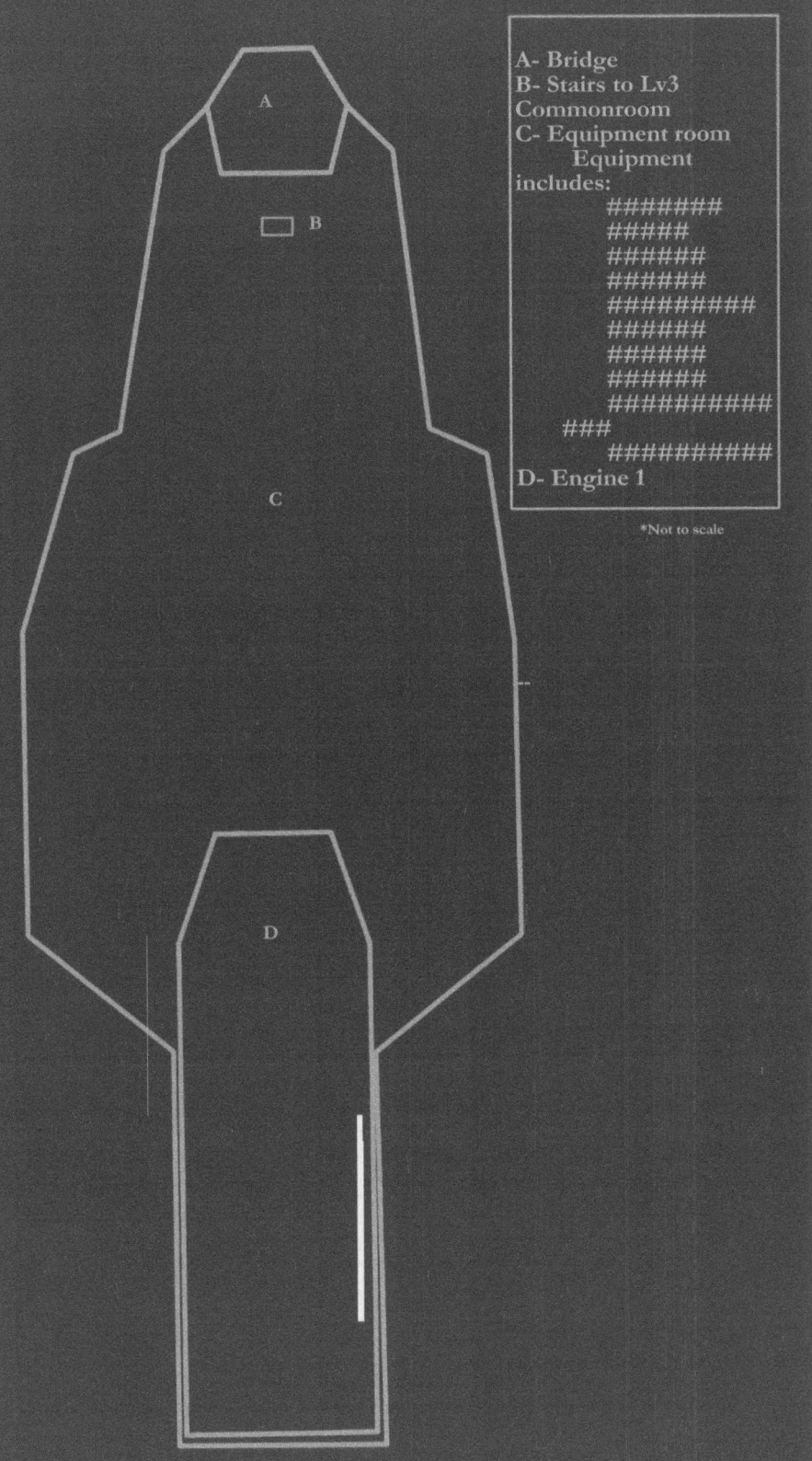

A- Bridge
B- Stairs to Lv3
Commonroom
C- Equipment room
    Equipment
includes:
        #######
        #####
        ######
        ######
        #########
        ######
        ######
        ######
        ##########
    ###
        #########
D- Engine 1

*Not to scale

Werewolf Level 4 - Inner hull and rooms

Beings from all over the galaxy filled the large corridor. Most were Terran, like Eric, but he found the vast range of subspecies unusual.

The smell of chemwash and engine grease was overpowering as he dodged past some of the slower moving groups in the crowd. Dirt, grease and the flaking of age stained the surrounding concrete. Some of its metal supports were visible. The metal grillwork that served as a floor, groaned under the constant weight of the passengers.

The flow of the crowd towards the centre of the space station was uneven. Just as it thinned out and the spaces between the groups widened, the floor-to-ceiling airlocks along the walls opened and more passengers emerged, packing the space as tight as before. The sounds of laughter, tears, and many languages in conversation filled the corridor.

Fencorns, with their cloven feet, clipped on the grillwork as they walked. Their tiny horns glinted in the uneven lighting around them.

Canis-types moved in small packs. The dog DNA spliced into them showed in their elongated faces, pointed teeth and fur on their heads.

A group of aliens passed through the crowd. Their multiple limbs reflecting oily colours as they moved constantly. Eric tried to avoid staring at them but found the movement of their extra joints fascinating. Behind them were large, worm-like creatures that left a trail of slime in their wake.

A team of cleanbots followed the cornucopia, chittering to themselves as they tried to remove the thick goo.

Eric's almost two-and-a-half metres of height made him taller than most of those around him. Over the heads of the crowd, he could see others leaning against the corridor walls in groups of four or more. They were not in a rush to leave the docks. Some had red sashes tied around their arms, denoting them as Sirius's security teams. Others had a cluster of lines tattooed on their throats, designating them as slaver gangs.

Running the advice from the ship's crew through his mind, he glanced at another group. They were devoid of any identifying marks. Bounty hunters. All of them carried rifles, gunbelts and the occasional cybernetic enhancement.

Adjusting the weight of his backpack, Eric tried to edge inconspicuously into the centre of the corridor. He hoped his calculated slow pace kept wandering eyes from being attracted to his movement.

He glanced down. Eric was rubbing at the almost invisible scar on his wrist. The harder skin ran from the centre of his palm and down over his wrist. It was only noticeable from the rest of his red-brown colouring when he touched it. And he only touched it when he had that prickle of unease or the chilly feeling of being watched.

Ahead of him, a tiny woman was carrying a young girl. Her cheek was pink as she lifted it off her mother's shoulder to stare at him. Pale grey, almost white, eyes were shining in the dimness. Her light frame and elongated features made her look more like an ethereal creature than a Terran child.

"Mummy, he looks funny."

The translator in his ear changed her words into his native tongue. Despite understanding her, Eric was not used to the more formal style of language it created.

At the girl's voice, the woman turned and tilted her chin sharply to look up at him. Eric smiled as she stammered an apology.

"Do not worry about it." As her own translator blinked in response to his words, Eric slowed a little more and leaned down to help with the large bag she was carrying. "I am probably a strange sight to a few people."

She smiled in return. "We have never seen so many subspecies," she admitted, as they moved further down the corridor. "Or aliens." She glanced about them at the crowd.

Eric followed her gaze, using the opportunity to check on those groups. They appeared more interested in the knots of people near them. The tightness in his shoulders eased a bit.

"You from Mars?"

His steps faltered as he processed the direct question.

In the time it took for him to recover, she had tensed. Sweat beaded her forehead and she glanced around them.

"The skin or the tattoos?" Eric ran his hand over his bald head at the mention of the ink there.

She relaxed a little and adjusted the girl on her shoulder. "Bit of both, I guess." They paused as the crowd grew too thick to navigate. "You?"

"Cantori Sector—one of the spacestations." She moved again, stopping almost directly under a light. Her skin reflected harshly.

Eric winced at its brightness. He shook his head while his eyes adjusted.

"We have family here," she added. The knot of people moved, allowing them to continue forward. "Decided things were good for a fresh start."

"Here?" Eric could not keep the surprise out of his tone. "On Sirius?"

"All spacestations need workers." The knowing look she gave Eric left him wordless for a moment. "Mechanics, electricians, cleaners. Even out here on The Rim. Without workers, things stop."

He nodded, her words pointing out to him what should have been obvious.

"Do you think they will have need of a cook?" Once he voiced it, Eric mulled over his question, tasting the words as something new, something unexpected. "To be honest, I had not really thought about what I would do once I got here."

"Few people do." She was looking away from him now, scanning the crowd around them as they moved closer to the core. "But..." she turned back to him, "you do not exactly look the part of a cook."

Eric shrugged and glanced at his hand, the scar felt by the tightness of his skin. "Got to have cooks on every planet, even Mars."

"Of course." She caught sight of something near the entrance to the core. Raising herself up on her toes, she waved.

Eric followed her gaze to see a small group of similar looking Terrans to her.

"Do yourself a favour." She took the bag from him and adjusted her daughter on her shoulder again. "Find someone who you trust to watch your back." She looked behind them down the corridor. "Solo travellers get dead fast out here."

"Thanks for the advice." Eric smiled at the little girl, barely hearing her mother's words. "Good luck with the fresh start."

"You too." She started heading towards her family, then stopped and turned to look at him one last time. "Thank you for helping. You kept us safe too."

Eric shook his head, laughing quietly at the accurate reading of his offered help. She hooked her bag over her free shoulder and nodded a farewell. The little girl waved at him. He returned the gesture before focusing on the path ahead and the words the mother had left him with.

He stepped out of the corridor into the core and moved to the side for a moment, processing the sight ahead. The entrance Eric walked through was not the only one. Around the ring, several large corridors spewed crowds into the core. The enormous space was a single layer in a large, many-levelled cylinder. The crowd flowed past, making their way to the elevators that ringed the edge of the walkway.

In the centre of the sphere was a large circular space that ran the length of the spacestation. Vehicles drove up and down in orderly lines. Landsleds, small transports and even some single motors hitched to platforms, were parked along the edge. Their drivers soliciting their rides to the passersby.

Against the outer wall, hawkers had set up small shops. Some were a mere table with some datachips, others with containers full of equipment and stock. There was even an eatery: Coolio's. The hamburgers sat in the warmer, slowly disintegrating from the grease in their meat.

Eric's stomach churned at the fatty smell as he walked closer to the wall and the sellers. He stepped near a small table and the merchant looked up at him.

The sound of a horn screamed through the noise of engines and people. Many heads turned towards the core. Other horns blared and transports scattered out of their lanes, as a red landsled wove through them. The blonde Terran at the controls oblivious to the responses of others as she twisted and turned the landsled at an insane speed.

"Crazies." The man behind the table muttered once the commotion settled. "If it wasn't for their money, the harbourmaster would toss the lot off the station."

Eric rubbed at his goatee, turning back to the Terran and his table full of parts. "The failure of the system." He shrugged. "Will not survive long driving like that, though."

The merchant returned the shrug and focused on Eric properly for the first time.

"New?"

"Fresh off the carrier." Eric glanced around. "Like most of those here, I imagine." He did not react as the man's face broke into a sly smile.

"Then you need a map." The Terran held up a chip, then pulled a chipreader out of his pocket and inserted it. A small hologram of the spacestation appeared above the screen.

"This little beauty connects directly to the mainframe of the station. It has continuous updates and tells you your location." He manipulated the image until it zoomed in to show a level of the core at the far edge of the lower levels. A single yellow beacon blinked at them. "Can throw in a chip of the local dialects too." He glanced at Eric's ear. "Your translator looks like it can cope with upgrades."

"How much?"

"Five trade credits."

Eric sighed and waved the item away. "Fresh off the carrier, remember? Only got UTC creds."

"Well, those aren't worth a lot out here." His smile got even wider. "It'll be 15 of those."

Eric looked at the map again, weighing up the need for the information against the hit to the credits he had. Deciding that it was worth the cost, he pulled a creditdisk out of his inner jacket pocket and slipped it through the offered cardreader.

The man nodded as the transaction went through.

"So," Eric watched the merchant put the reader away, "who will you get to change those credits over?"

The merchant's sly look reappeared. "Wondering who to trust?"

"Do not want it to be too obvious I am fresh off the carrier."

He laughed quietly at Eric's counter and pointed along the wall to a woman several stalls away.

"That's Janice. She will give you a fair trade of UTC creds." He winked. "She will make money, no doubt about that, but she will not gouge the life blood from you or tell the local press gang what you are carrying. Some of us still have a code here. Unlike those crazies on the trade levels."

"Thanks." Eric nodded a farewell and headed towards Janice. He waited as she served a few of the slug looking aliens. She seemed to know them, laughing at their strange clicks. Eric pulled his translator out of his ear and clipped the small chip into a slot. By the time he had fitted it back comfortably, Janice was looking at him.

"Yes?" Her tone and expression were neutral as she looked up at him.

Eric haggled exchange rates with her for a few minutes. Happy with their deal, he headed towards the elevator, not really knowing where exactly he was going but deciding that it was safer to keep moving. Joining the end of a group, he got into the next one that arrived. His nose crinkled as the acrid smell of chemwash from them all intensified in the enclosed space.

He checked the control panel near the closing doors. It had three options written in the Terran language, known as Trade: *Docks, Residential* and *Trade*.

Eric braced himself as the elevator powered on. He could see the scratches in the tough plastic windows. They quivered from the force of the air passing outside. Hundreds of levels flew by, all filled with thousands of beings.

The elevator slowed then stopped at the residential levels. Most of the crowd got out, giving those left some room.

Eric pulled the chipreader out again as the elevator headed up through the core, towards the trade levels. He opened the map, noting the landing level of the elevator he was in. A single bar took up most of it. The map called it Rebeal, and a note advised it was currently closed for repairs.

Eric skimmed the layout of the rest of the area. A cave-like structure of winding pathways and shops spilt over the floor and two mezzanines. He powered the chipreader down and slipped it back into his pocket. Readjusting the strap of his backpack, he leaned against the wall and watched the levels go past.

As Eric stepped out of the elevator and onto the trade level, there was another sizeable crowd. Instead of the groups all heading towards the one goal of leaving, this level was full of browsers. Shops and small eateries lined the main core. Between them, many dark corridors led into the maze that promised food, equipment and other unidentified needs that were serviced in the shadows.

The constant hum of conversation gave Eric a sense of familiarity. Different to all the trade sectors he had known, the white noise of talking, eating and browsing also had the thrill of danger, with the open display of guns and weapons on nearly everyone he saw.

He rubbed the scar on his wrist again, resisting the urge to wipe his hand on the side of his hip from the sweat on his palms.

Overlooking the space was a large three-storey black wall. Made of glass-style material, someone had painted it with the same word over and over in many languages: *Rebeal*.

The florescent green paint glowed slightly, directing Eric's eyes to a pair of doors in the middle. On the doors, someone had painted a stylised Terran hand, its image giving the bird to passersby. As he watched, the doors slid open and two Terrans stumbled out. Behind them, he glimpsed a large crowd.

"Thought it was closed," Eric muttered, his hand brushing the pocket containing his map.

The edge of the walkway had more bays for the landsleds. Eric shook his head, recognising the faded paint and dented panels of the red vehicle from earlier.

"Interested in some company?"

A set of long fingers slid around Eric's forearm and he shivered. He looked down at the breasts pressed against his side. A forked tail wrapped around his thigh, its tip curving up to wiggle between his legs and against his crotch.

The Fencorn smiled at him, revealing white teeth and a pair of short fangs between blood-red lipstick. The colour of her lips matched her horns to the tint, as they poked out of her long black hair.

Eric opened his mouth to speak but paused, inhaling her scent of clean skin and perfume.

"Just got here, did you?" she added in a low tone.

Eric squirmed, his pants suddenly feeling far too tight.

"It is that obvious?" he counted.

She smiled at him, letting her hair fall over her face as she angled her head, considering his words. "It is the smell that gives you away."

"Yeah… Speaking of that, do you know of a clean bunking station?" His stomach tightened at the suggestive look on her face and the slightly harder stroke from her tail.

"You get free lodgings with us, including showers… If you buy the service." The incline of her head lessened and her fingers flexed. "But it is only for the duration."

Eric tried to untangle himself from her tail. He breathed in her scent again, tasting the pheromones she was giving off as a sweet delicacy. "Maybe later…"

She pouted at him but withdrew a little, giving Eric clear air while her fingers slid off his arm.

"Head down that way." She pointed towards one corridor. "Down the end of the row, there is a place called Death's End. They have filtered water showers." She winked at him. "I am working all night."

Eric glanced at the tight black dress she wore that hid nothing. "Thanks."

She grabbed his arm as he went to move.

"Watch your back shoulders." She smiled. "Lots of people around here will like what you have got." She cupped the back of his thigh, feeling the tight muscles.

His leg jolted at her touch, his body warming.

"Do not forget the way back and ask for Kei." She waved at him and turned to a small group he had not noticed near her. They laughed and joked with her about something Eric did not catch. She shrugged them off with a flick of her wrist and tail.

Eric gave Kei a last look before heading in the direction she had indicated. A certain amount of regret and temptation swirled through his thoughts. His skin was crawling at the suggestion of danger, but instinct told him she was not the threat.

The corridor closed in around him, quickly muffling the general hum of transports from the core. Built out of large storage crates, the corridors and shops were haphazard in their layout, with one corridor merging with another, then splitting at odd angles.

He glanced at a few food stores but dismissed enquiring at them when he caught glimpses of the tiny workspaces or the Terran-shaped cuts hanging to cure. The smells of cooking meat filled the air, tinged with the acrid scent of the slightly rotting.

Eric's stomach protested at the change, leaving him to think even more favourably about Kei's scent and her offer.

As he moved further into the complex of corridors and containers, the ambient light darkened, turning his vision into the more contrasting greys that enabled him to see better in the shadows.

It did not take long for Eric to notice the man tailing him. His metal arm shone, reflecting fragments of dim light as he moved around through the knots of people at the edge of Eric's vision. The large rifle the man carried looked flashy but bulky and hard to manoeuvre in the tight space of the corridor.

Anger edged Eric's thoughts as he noticed the slaver tattoos on his neck.

Near a larger intersection of four corridors, Eric slowed to look at the equipment in a shop front. He used the time to take in the man's position and to see if they were alone.

The old Terran merchant glanced at Eric, then turned back to the customer he was serving. A Kat was fingering a chipset on the table, as if she was assessing it and the price quoted. Her striped, grey fur was slick in the light. Her ears flickered back and forth, listening to people around her, but her slitted blue eyes never left the chip in her hand. In her left ear, a commlink's light flickered green and yellow.

"Slavers," she snarled. An angry hiss followed the word, her claws poking out of their sheaths on her fingers.

The word created a surge of adrenaline in Eric. Exhaling slowly, he forced his muscles to remain relaxed. He edged closer to the table, looking at equipment parts laid out in front of him, watching the Kat from the edge of his vision.

"They followed me."

"Seven, Martian." The ears flickered. "Two at each entrance and one behind... Gerdy?"

The old man nodded.

"Go right." She flexed a hand, the light shining down the length of her claws.

The merchant dropped behind his table and the Kat twisted, leaping off to the left, back towards the corridor Eric had walked down. He turned towards the nearest entrance, glancing around.

The hum of guns powering up was impossibly loud in the suddenly empty corridor.

Eric turned and dodged the outstretched arm of the nearest slaver, before slamming his fist into their face. He ripped the handgun from their grip. Settling it into his palm, he turned and fired at the pair in the far corridor. After cycles of inactivity and being couped up on the spaceship, his sudden decisive action was an explosion of speed and force.

The pair ducked for cover as he closed the space between him and a woman. Her legs whirled with gears as she turned, her rifle point swinging towards him.

Eric smashed the butt of the handgun into her nose. Blood spurted everywhere as he stepped behind her. Her scream rung in his ear. Several energy bullets thudded into her body. Reaching around her, Eric pointed the rifle in her hand towards the others and crushed her fingers as he pulled the trigger.

The two slavers dropped from his energy bullets, groaning as they grasped at burn wounds on their chests and sides.

He glanced towards the Kat. She had downed the man carrying the large rifle. Her compact figure straddling his chest, she dug her claws into the sides of his face.

Following Eric's gaze, the last two slavers looked at the scene, cursed, and bolted. Eric noticed a flicker in the shadows that looked like another Kat following them.

Gasping for air, Eric's heart slowed as he looked around. He let go of the rifle and stepped away from the woman, letting her body fall to the ground. He lowered his hand.

Muscles felt heavy as he processed the sight of the dead Terrans. Blood darkened the faces of the two near him, their vacant eyes stared into nothingness. The smell of three types of bodily functions thickened the air.

"Never could keep myself out of trouble," he muttered, flexing his fingers around the handgun and stepping toward the Kat.

She leaned back, her ears twisting towards Eric as she checked the man's pockets. The slaver's eyes stared blankly at the ceiling. Blood seeped from the ten puncture wounds across his face, but his chest moved under her. She purred as she found something and slipped it into the small bag that hung from a thin shoulder strap.

"You ok?" Eric tried to keep the caution out of his tone but failed.

The Kat turned and smiled at him. She then stood, dusting her fur off. Her eyes blurred as the commlink in her ear flashed, the tiny blue light blinking, and her ears folded again. Her tail sunk down between her legs.

"Captain." As she spoke, she held a claw against the device's button. She looked up at Eric. "Acknowledged." She stretched her paw out to the wall.

Eric winced at the sharp sound her claws made as she dragged them across the surface, cleaning them. Blood smeared along the wall in their wake.

"You know how to use that?" she asked, nodding at the gun in Eric's hand.

"Yeah." Eric opened his palm, looking at the black metal of the gun. He moved to throw it away.

"Keep it."

"You do not have one."

She shrugged at him. "I have other weapons." She motioned back towards the main area of the level. "This way."

Eric glanced back at the sound of something heavy being lifted.

The old merchant, Gerdy, was dragging a corpse into his shop.

"This is not the place for new arrivals to linger." Her ears turned at a noise he did not hear and Eric followed her around the corner. There was a muffled gun blast behind him.

"That obvious?" Eric laughed quietly, reaching the Kat's side.

She looked up at him, her ear partially folded back.

"Bag, smell of chemwash… heading to Death's End."

He pulled on the straps of his backpack.

"How did…" Eric inhaled as the thought occurred to him.

She shook her head. "No. The grillwalkers did not set you up. The press gangs figured out their recommendations to the new arrivals and follow the unsuspecting."

"And you?"

"Do not like slavers."

"That is not what—"

"Do yourself a favour," she cut him off, "get off the publics as fast as you can."

"I was trying to." He paused, his foot mid-step as she turned and raised an eyebrow at him.

"I do not mean finding a place to stay. Get a crew, a job… Anything. Someone to watch your back." Her ears twisted towards the corridor they came from. "If you want to live, that is."

Eric rubbed at his scalp.

"Know anyone looking for a cook?" He waited while she assessed him again.

"Cook?" She focused on the gun in his hand. "If you say so." She tapped her chin with a claw. "Ask at Rebeal. Sasha, the head chef, is always looking for staff. But…" She motioned to the gun. "Hide that."

He saw the blue light flicker on her commlink again.

She activated it with a fingerpad. "Yes, Captain." She smiled at Eric. "I need to go. Remember though, Rebeal's owner is Custurian. Do not mess with the alcohol. Can you find your way?"

Eric nodded, flicking the safety onto the handgun and tucking it into his pants at the small of his back.

She pounced onto all fours, turned once to nod at him, then sped off into the crowd.

"Thanks," Eric said to the empty air.

He retraced his path to the core and Rebeal, replaying the scene in his mind. The handgun felt heavy against the small of his back with the backpack pressing it into his spine.

Eric looked up at the solid black wall when he reached Rebeal's sliding doors. He rolled his shoulders and stepped through them. The doors shut behind him.

He glanced around the bar and over the heads of the patrons in front of him. There was a definite strangeness to the place. It was too quiet compared to the size of the crowd he could see under the multicoloured lights.

To his right, a metal counter ran the width of the space. Behind it, the wall was three stories of shelving with liquid-filled containers of every colour. Robotic arms shifted up and down the wall, depositing and removing them at the direction of the staff below.

The humanoids behind the bar had blue-tinged translucent skin that glowed slightly as they served the patrons with long, thin tentacles. Smaller tentacles wriggled on their chins along with the soft tops of their heads as they spoke.

As he continued to the back of the bar, Eric noticed a brownish humanoid waving its tentacles about, with one jabbing towards the datascreens on the far wall. A group of beings crowded this area.

He recognised several Most Wanted Lists from various universal powers and screens full of betting odds. Under them were two sets of doors. To his left were two mezzanine levels packed with tables and chairs full of Terrans and aliens drinking, eating, and talking. Everyone had a betting device blinking on them.

A space opened in front of him. A deep crimson pool was spreading over the floor, the body of a Terran male at the centre. His corpse was twisted unnaturally, eyes staring blankly at the ceiling. Several large slashes in his neck, thighs and ribs seeped more blood.

"Quick shower." An arm accompanied the low and familiar female tone, sliding around his.

Eric looked down at soft breasts pressed against his upper arm. Dark crimson eyes stared up at him while a tail wrapped around his thigh. Eric cleared his throat as the smell of pheromones left it dry.

"I'm looking for Sasha." Eric swallowed, his pants feeling restrictive again.

"Why Sasha?" Kei smiled. The fingers of her free hand slid up the back of his thigh to grope his arse.

"Been told to ask her about a job." Eric caught the tail, trying to untangle it from his leg.

"Bouncer?"

"Cook." Eric rolled his eyes at her sceptical look. "For real."

"Cook?" Her smile widened as her fingers brushed the handgun at his back. "If you say so." The tail unwrapped, and she pulled her hand out from under his jacket.

Eric breathed easier, the scent lessening.

"This way."

The Fencorn directed Eric towards the doors at the edge of the bar. She glanced at the body as they passed. Some people and cleanbots were already hard at work.

"What happened?"

"Xion finally put his foot in it." She watched as some men took the body out of one of the rear doors.

"Ok… What killed him?" Eric raised his eyebrows as she looked up at him.

"Not what." Her laughter was harsh. "Although have heard her called worse things. Most, however, call her Hawke."

"Hawke?" Eric rubbed his neck. "Sounds familiar…"

"She captains the Werewolf." Kei pointed to the large datascreens on the wall they were approaching.

Eric looked up at them. The United Trade Confederates' top ten MWL was on one of the largest screens. Number eight was the listing, *Hauk, Pirate Captain* and their ship, *Werewolf.*

Eric turned back to Kei, catching her tail and removing it from his leg again as they reached the door.

"Just so you know," she knocked, her tail sliding in his grip and wiggling against his crotch, "staff get free service."

"There's no meat in this?" Sasha asked before she tasted the stew. Her clothes were neat but showed a person who was not afraid to get in and do the work from the grease stains and blobs of food on her apron.

Eric vaguely recalled descriptions of the golden-skinned, green-eyed Centaurians as fierce fighters. Although Sasha had the colouring, the image she projected was far from a soldier. She had strength in her muscles but not in the way that suggested combat training. Her cropped short hair and an implant that replaced her right eye, did not fit with Sasha's tall, wide frame.

"You watched me make it." Eric motioned towards the bench covered with leftover ingredients.

She watched him for a moment before having a second taste. "It needs more spice, but not bad."

"More spice?"

"We like our flavour in Rebeal." Sasha smiled and put the spoon down. "Our food is known for it." She pointed to the back of the kitchen and another set of doors. "We also have safe living quarters for our staff. We dislike losing people to… What do they call themselves? Recruitment teams."

Eric set his shoulders and jaw at the mention of slavers.

"I see you have already met some of them." Sasha smiled again, and Eric nodded in reply, not trusting his voice. "Well, you know to be wary outside of Rebeal, then." She indicated towards the door. "Find a bunk and take a shower… You stink of chemwash."

"Better than the alternative."

It took a moment for Sasha to react to Eric's smile. She nodded, but her eyes narrowed a little as she considered him.

"Only just," she agreed. "My rules are simple: do your job and do not get into fights." Her tone was firm.

"Yes, Chef."

"Got a name?"

Eric opened his mouth but paused. In his mind, the large datascreen of the UTC MWLs appeared. He breathed deeply, calming his nerves before answering. "Jon."

"Ok, Jon." Sasha straightened, launching into what sounded like a well-rehearsed speech. "The harbourmaster set Sirius to Terran Standard time when he bought the station. We run on eight-hour standards, two off and one on shift. Your shift standard will change every 28 rotations, four sequences or one cycle... They are all the same. I honestly do not care what you call them."

She paused, watching Eric until he nodded in understanding.

"The dwarf sun we orbit has a pathetic three-cycle revolution, so we just use the 13 cycles in a Sol revolution—I am assuming you are familiar with those?"

Eric bit his tongue at the thought he was from the Sol system. "Yes, Chef."

"Kei." Sasha never raised her voice but within seconds, a tail wrapped itself around Eric's thigh and fingers slid around his forearm. "Show Jon where he can find a spare bunk. There's a dirty clothes bin in the commonroom for the apron. Clean ones are there too for the start of every shift."

Sasha turned from them and called over a kitchenhand, directing her to take the stew to the staff commonroom.

"This way." Kei handed Eric his backpack and folded jacket.

He felt the weight of the handgun in the folds of the material. She led him out of the kitchen and into a darkened warehouse. He glanced around at all the boxes and several cold rooms as they wove through the packed space.

"Boss likes his alcohol where he can see it is not being tampered with." Kei shrugged at Eric's frown. "He is one of those Custurians that worship the stuff." She rolled her eyes. "Know a few Terrans that should convert."

"Where do you fit in?" Eric swallowed, watching Kei as she walked ahead.

"Booze, food and sex." She laughed, wiggling her arse in its tight skirt. "Everything you need. Now, you tell me." She looked back at him as she reached another set of doors. "How does someone who just arrived know the head chef's name?"

"Yeah…" He rubbed his goatee. "Lucky, I guess."

They entered a large room full of chairs and long tables. Several beings, mainly Terrans, were sitting about, eating or murmuring. In the far corner, at the back of the room, was a kitchenette. Next to that, a door to a set of stairs and an elevator.

"Commonroom," Kei said, then pointed at a container that was the clothes bin.

Eric dropped the apron into it before following her to the stairwell. As they climbed the levels, he told her about the encounter with the slavers and the Kat.

Kei's hooves clicked on the metal steps, her hair bouncing in time.

"Lucky." She stopped at a landing, rolled the word around on her tongue, then looked back at him.

Warmth spread across Eric's body from the tones in her voice. His skin prickled and felt chilled as he got that hunted feeling again.

"And good timing."

"Timing?" Eric watched Kei put a finger against her chin, tapping it.

"Well…" Kei moved closer to him, her tail wrapping around his thigh again. Her finger now tracked the edges of the tattoo across his forehead, going down towards an ear. "I need a new bunkmate."

She smiled at Eric's slightly guarded expression. He swallowed, deeply breathing in her hormones.

"You are going to get more than one offer." She ran her finger over his jaw and his muscles tightened. "We all like something new here."

"Something?" Eric's eyebrows raised. "Intriguing way to put it."

The look she fixed him with made Eric uncomfortable. The combination of arousal and vigilance was new. It stirred excitement in his gut he could not admit he missed in the past cycles.

"At least check the space out before you reject it for a mattress on the commonroom floor."

Eric nodded, and she led the way down the corridor and through the door.

The room was small, just large enough for a bed, a table, and a small set of cupboards in the corner. The bed was messy and tiny, bright-coloured underwear hung from the cupboard knobs. Another door led to a small wet room.

"It is not much, but it is secure." Kei slid onto the table, facing him.

"You shared this?"

"Different shifts." Kei shrugged, her tail doing lazy loops behind her again. "Only occasionally shared the bed."

"Why did they leave?" Eric put his bag and jacket down next to her, watching her face as she spoke.

"Dana finally got her shit together and left." Kei's legs dangled as she grabbed the edge of the table, pushing her breasts up.

Eric looked at the wet room, feeling short of breath. The pheromones thickened the air again.

"She always talked of going off to one of the freehold planets in the Xidinan solar system." Kei shrugged and Eric rubbed the back of his neck. "No turning it off." Her laughter was rich in the small space. "Does help when negotiating, though."

"Then maybe I should take a—" He stopped as she rolled her eyes, shaking her head. Her long black hair slid over her shoulders in waves, and Eric had a powerful urge to stroke it.

"You'll wake up with one of us on you and another three waiting for their turn." She inclined her head as he considered that. "Unless you like that idea?"

"Well... it has been a while." Eric returned her smile with his own. "Maybe I would."

Her tongue flickered over her sharp canines.

"But I think I need a shower before I consider anything other than a long sleep in an actual bed." He groaned as she stretched her legs out, showing off the bright red underwear she wore. "You are pushing..."

"Think of it as a roommate interview." Kei put a finger to her lips, smiling at his reaction. "I need to make sure you are suitable."

"Suitable?" Eric paused only a moment before that feeling below his gut decided for him.

He inhaled her scent. Closing the gap between them, he moved closer. Kei spread her legs, giving him room.

She looked up at him, sticking her finger into her mouth, sucking on it.

He felt her knees press against his thighs and she leaned back. His fingers tingled as he ran them up her legs, enjoying the feel of her smooth skin.

She gripped his shoulder with one hand, running her wet finger down her neck to her chest.

Leaning forward, Eric breathed in the pheromones, his eyes following her finger.

Kei unzipped her dress slowly down the front, exposing the red bra she wore underneath.

Eric pressed his smile against her skin, then ran his tongue under the edge of the material on her chest. Kei gasped, pushing a clothed breast into his mouth on instinct. He continued down, following the path of the zipper. His hands slid up to her hips.

"Yes," she murmured, leaning further back.

He moved his hands just enough to slip her panties down her legs. He massaged her crotch, finding her wet already. His mouth moved back to her covered tit.

Kei's moans became excited squeals. Her thighs ground against him as his fingers moved with long, soft strokes.

Eric pulled away just as he felt her tense. His belt and pants dropped easily while she helped him pull his top off.

"Do it." She reached for his hips, pulling him towards her.

The air grew heavy. The hint of sweetness was tantalising.

Eric felt the rising heat and welcomed the tight feeling in his belly. He leaned over her, touching his tip to her slit.

Kei's eyes widened, and she glanced down, her fingers wrapping around his shaft.

"Oh… Yes." She stroked him, angling her hips.

Eric eased in, penetrating slowly, enjoying the feeling of her surrounding him, pressing against him. A half groan, half sigh came from him as he felt her push forward a little, encasing him completely.

"Let's get this interview going," he whispered into her ear, his hands gripping her arse. She moaned in answer as Eric started thrusting.

The kitchen was full of workers. Having spent the last few sequences at Rebeal, the general conversations and the spicy smells of food cooking were familiar to Eric. He slid a platter of food onto the serving bench and tapped the button to alert the waiting staff.

As Eric turned to head back to his station, a group of servers entered from the bar doors. They stopped, ignoring the serving bench and gathered into a corner, away from the others. Their almost fearful expressions made Eric's skin tingle, putting him on alert.

"What is going on?" Sasha demanded, appearing from behind Eric. "Food needs to be served, people."

"Chef," one server, a female, spoke up as the others closed ranks behind her, "couple of the gangs are going at each other out there..."

The alarms went off in everyone's translators, bringing the conversation to a halt. Linked to the communication infrastructure of the bar, the devices allowed for silent notifications across the security system. The sounds going off in Eric's ear still had him on edge as he learned to translate the pings and dings into words.

"Stardust." Sasha growled a little at the alarm. "A few sequences with none of the Brethren in dock and they all grow cocks larger than they can hold." She waved her hand, dismissing Eric's surprised look at hearing her curse. "Fine. Give it a few minutes to calm—"

The alarm pierced Eric's ear drum, rebounding in his head. It took a few seconds to translate: someone had attacked one or some of the Rebeal grillwalkers.

"Kei." Eric stepped towards the doors leading out into the main bar, but Sasha caught his forearm in a powerful grip, bringing him to a stop.

"She has survived longer than you out here, Jon." Her eyes narrowed as he turned back to her. "That need you have, to go looking for trouble, get rid of it. No fighting."

"Chef, I…"

"I mean it." She inhaled then sighed, releasing his arm.

From the bar, they could hear the yells of the bouncers and the steady thump of their electrified pacifier rods. A few more of the servers burst through the doors and joined the others. Their excited voices describing the scenes to those in the kitchen and almost drowning out the activity of the fight itself.

"That is enough." Sasha's voice boomed across the room. The other conversations died in its echoes. "It is being handled." She continued at a lower volume. "Why the dramatics?"

"Sorry, Chef." One of the huddled servers spoke up.

Eric recognised Dante. The Canis fur on their scalp was a bright pink and matched carefully with their lipstick and tunic under the Rebeal apron. "Last time these two gangs had words, Captain Denthar and his crew stepped in… Remember that?"

"That scrap?" Sasha rolled her eyes and motioned to Eric to return to his station.

"Chef?" Eric knew his curiosity was showing and he did not care. He had one ear focused on the noise coming from outside.

"Do you understand why I have the rule, no fighting?" She fixed him with an intense gaze and Eric nodded slowly.

"Keeps us off the hit lists." Eric gritted his teeth, not adding it was the perfect cover and protection.

Sasha sighed, rolling her shoulders. "Denthar and his crew aren't bad, not as the brethren go. When a few of the staff got caught in the crossfire, he respected us enough to step in and protect them." She smiled a little. "I also think he took out a few marks for himself as well."

There were a few shouts and several large thumps against the wall. Eric's fists clenched, but he remained where he was.

She noticed his reaction, dropping the smile into a frown. "For a Martian, you are far too ready to take people on."

"And what if they ever go for the staff?" Eric straightened his fingers with an effort. "I mean, use them?"

She blinked as his question sunk in, then understanding spread across her face.

"I see." She tapped his datascreen, bringing up the next few orders as the noise outside lessened. "We have the security team to do that—and only that. They stay out of the fighting unless the staff or the alcohol get threatened. If anyone, I mean anyone, goes for our staff, they step in. If you feel the need, take that apron off and hand it over."

The orders on the screen blinked and several struck off the To-Make list.

"That's why customers pay in advance here. You could have been making those... I really dislike the waste." She paused as the all-clear trilled through their translators. There was an impatience to her voice when she turned to see that the group of servers had not moved. "Someone take that platter to..." She looked at Eric.

"48." Eric watched the servers turn to each other, waiting for the first one to make the move. "I'll take it, Chef."

Sasha watched him for a moment, then nodded.

Eric picked up the platter and made his way through the kitchen doors towards the patrons. He weaved through the crowd.

People looked at him, saw the apron and the platter, and turned away. Their disinterest surprised him and he exhaled slowly, his body relaxing. He slipped the platter onto table 48, tapped the coding into the table's control pad and headed straight back towards the kitchen doors.

They had already cleaned up the main area, any evidence of the fight gone. Several of the Custurian wives were replacing a few alcohol bottles on the upper shelves of the bar. From the glistening liquid and the shattered glass on the floor, Eric summarised that some of the stock had not survived.

A few cleanbots were already working on the mess. He saw the owner standing in the doorway to the storage room, yelling at someone on the other side. His brown skin was translucent with anger, tentacles jabbing at the air.

"He should be used to it by now."

Eric felt his shoulders relax as familiar fingers slid around his forearm. He looked down at Kei who was pressed against his side.

He draped an arm over her shoulders. She leaned in closer to talk in his ear and they headed back to the kitchen.

"You ok?" Eric's breath caught as he smelled, then saw, the blood in her hair and on her clothes.

She smiled at him, attempting to wipe at it, smearing the blood across her cheek.

"Some dick took his slave roleplay too seriously." She shook her head. "If he really wanted to abuse someone that bad, he could have found an owner out on the publics that sells those goods. But then his crew tried to defend him."

She blinked when Eric stopped walking, his entire body tensing. "Hope he got some bottle shards up his arse."

"Jon, you are not that naïve."

"No." He forced a smile that they both knew he did not mean and continued towards the kitchen, his arm still wrapped around her. "I just hate it when some people think they can do what they want to others."

He moved intentionally slow, wanting a little extra time with her. "The customer?"

"Currently looking for a container doctor to reattach his balls." She showed Eric the blood under her long nails.

Eric chuckled. "One of these rotations I will remember not to get worried about you."

Kei pouted. "Do not do that." She transitioned into her seductive tone and expression effortlessly. "I like it." She tapped his shoulder in a signal for him to let her go. "Got to go check on the others. Some of them are still new enough to be surprised at security's response."

"And that was?"

"Making sure he needed to get the arm reattached too."

With a hand on the kitchen door, Eric watched her go. He did not know why he felt the need to follow her. He shook his head, pushed his shoulders back and headed to his prep table, ignoring the curious looks from Sasha and a few other cooks.

Rebeal felt unusually crowded under the mezzanines for Eric during this shift. He pushed past a few of the loitering groups and headed for one of the gaming tables. Able to hold the platter at shoulder height and keep it above most of the customers' heads, he avoided the trouble the regular servers were having.

Four Terrans were playing cards as he slid the food onto a clear spot on their table and pressed the delivery code into the service panel. One man glanced up at him, then did a double take.

After several cycles in Rebeal, Eric was used to the reaction to his size, or skin, or tattoos and ignored the look, remaining focused on the panel. It pinged acceptance of the code.

He continued to disregard the man's reaction as he nudged the cyborg sitting next to him.

A small twinge between Eric's shoulder blades nagged at him and he turned back towards the bar.

All around him, the groups looked a little more huddled than normal, as if they did not want any individual singled out. There was a weird charge in the air, a tense expectation, which he had not felt before.

A few regulars had situated themselves to the far back of the space into the darker corners, not their usually preferred spots at the bar. The atmosphere set Eric's nerves tingling.

Glancing around, his heartbeat rose in tempo. It was like everyone expected something to happen, but no one seemed to want to start it.

Once Eric reached the edge of the mezzanine overhang, the crowd cleared, leaving the space between him and the bar almost empty. Several people were leaning against the large counter, talking to each other as they waited for their orders.

Near the kitchen entrance, Kei was sitting alone. She was reclining against the bar, her chin resting on her palm. Staring at the long glass in front of her, she swirled the bright yellow liquid with a straw.

"Shift almost over?"

Her eyes were dull as she looked up at the sound of Eric's voice. Her hair was rat-tailed with damp and her tail did lazy loops behind her. Even her pheromones lacked their normal intensity. She sat up a little taller, her tail finding his thigh.

"Yeah." She dropped her hands to the bar, the metal of the table clanking slightly. "Been a long shift. No one's buying this rotation. You?"

"Soon." He looked around the bar again. That nagging feeling refused to go. The skin at back of his neck tingled. "I will be glad to get out of here. Something feels off… Chef's having a tough time getting the food out to the tables."

Kei half laughed, half grunted, her tail finding its way up his back and over a forearm. She stood from her stool and pressed against him. "Everyone gets edgy when she first arrives."

Eric leaned back to look at Kei's face, but she was looking past him and along the wall to the far back corner of the room. Her eyes were shining in the glow of the lights, a tiny smile on her face. Turning to follow her line of sight, he noticed a single table with almost clear space around it.

"The original Brethren, Captain Hawke." Kei's whisper had the hint of admiration and more than a little awe.

Facing them, two grey tabby Kats sat at a table with a blonde, female Terran. The larger of the Kats, a male, sat unnaturally straight. His movements, as he raised a drink to his mouth, were precise and economical. His ears flickered back and forth as he listened to the general hum of the bar.

The female Kat next to him almost lounged in her seat. Her knees leaned against the table, and one of her arms hung over the back of her chair. She stretched and turned towards something near the main entrance as the male Kat said something.

The female Terran with them leaned back in her chair against the wall behind her. She took a large drink from her glass as the Kats conversed.

Eric noted how, even sitting, she was clear of the table, able to stand with no need to shift the chair away first. Her heavy, well-worn, black jacket was dull in the poor lighting of Rebeal. The pair of handguns in her thigh holsters, however, showed the most use.

"Is she that dangerous?" Eric recognised the hallmarks of a fighter, yet she did not seem to be like some of the real crazies who came in—those the security teams had tails on from the moment they entered the bar until they left. Or, someone that would justify the change in the entire bar's atmosphere.

Kei tensed, turning back to him, then smiled. "That's right. You walked in after Xion."

A tingle ran down his spine as he remembered the rotation he had arrived at Sirius several cycles before, and the dead body on Rebeal's floor.

"She would rather get bloodied after a raid than the usual booze and sex."

Eric continued to watch the table, focusing on the female Kat. "Funny you mention that rotation. Remember that story I told you about the Kat?"

"Kat?" Kei stiffened a little, then smiled again. "The one sitting there... Was that her?"

Eric nodded.

Kei turned to the bar and signalled to the Custurian owner. "Whiskey for Captain Hawke."

He handed a tumbler to Eric. Full to the brim, the amber liquid refracted the dull warm lights of the bar as it dropped a little in Eric's grip. He winced when he noticed there was no ice for dilution.

"Come on, I will introduce you." Kei jumped down to the floor and started walking towards Hawke's table. She stopped, looked back, and motioned with her tail for Eric to follow.

When he reached her, she whispered, "No perving, groping, or suggesting. You will end up like Xion if you do."

"So, nothing you have been teaching me, then?" He smiled and her eyes narrowed.

"I mean it." Her tone was sharp and her tail jittered with nerves.

He looked back at the table, reassessing its three occupants. The Kats did not seem to faze Kei, unlike the captain.

As they approached, the male Kat said something Eric could not hear.

The female Kat turned around to watch him and Kei as they approached. Her ears folded slightly. She then swivelled in the chair, kneeling on the seat as she leaned her arms on the back.

"Captain." The Kat's voice had the air of warning, her whiskers quivering.

"Little fuckin hard not to see him, Con."

Hawke's deep voice carried a tone of command and, Eric noted, amusement. There was the tiniest curve to her mouth, confirming this thought. Her yellow eyes reflected the lights oddly, almost like mirrors, but they did not hide the intent gaze focused on him.

Kei nudged him in the ribs and pointed at the glass in his hand.

"Captain," he greeted her, putting the glass on the table within arm's reach.

Eric matched her gaze with his, noticing the captain's hair was more gold than blonde and, in its high ponytail, completely unbrushed. Her jacket looked even older and more worn up close, marred with damage. One shoulder had a hammered metal patch that was singed dark from energy burns and scratches.

Even the equipment containers on her gunbelt and the spare gun batteries appeared tarnished and dented. Above the collar of her jacket, he could see stylised feathers tattooed in black on her neck.

"Do not mind the captain." The male Kat stood up from his chair and leaned over the table to extend a paw-like hand. "I am Chris."

Eric took the offered hand. He heard the gears as Chris's pawed fingers closed carefully around his palm. Metal claws poked out from the pads slightly but the Kat was careful to not let them near Eric's skin. Focusing on the Kat's eyes, Eric saw mechanics instead of slitted irises.

"I believe you have met my sister, Coni." Chris smiled, dipping his head towards her, an ear twisting in that direction, then released Eric's hand and motioned to the Terran. "And this is Captain Hawke."

Eric noticed the lights running across Chris's eyes as he looked up at the datascreens on the wall.

"Eight on the UTC, six on the Alati MWLs," Chris said with an air of listing simple facts. "For now."

"Jon." Eric felt an icy shiver run down his spine at the mention of those MWLs. He had largely forgotten about them during these past cycles.

Hawke snorted, causing the group to turn and look at her. She was still staring at Eric, her arms crossed, head tilted, reminding him of the bird of prey she shared her name with.

He was certain he saw that smile again. He turned towards the Kats and looked at Coni.

"Captain, I think he might be even taller than you." Coni smiled, looking up at Eric.

He felt the purring before he heard it.

"Martians grow like fuckin greens." Hawke snatched the tumbler from the table.

Coni's ears flattened at her captain's sharp words.

The purring stopped as a burst of activity erupted around them, with the sound of chairs scraping along the floor and guns being drawn in the charged quiet of Rebeal.

Eric glanced around. Some patrons stood up from their tables, while others reached for their weapon, fingers stopping on the grips or pulling them half out of holsters before pausing.

Hawke's sharp laughter was quiet, almost silent, as she lifted the drink to her lips. The sound sent chills down Eric's spine. She drank before resting the tumbler on the inside of her elbow. Not once taking her gaze from him.

The surrounding movement settled slowly. Eric looked around again, realising she had deliberately baited those watching her. That icy chill settled like a vice around his ribs and he picked up on the captain's readiness, but also her relaxed, almost flippant, attitude. As if those around them did not threaten her in the slightest. He inclined his head at Hawke. She nodded in return.

"Coni," Eric said, turning back to the Kat, "thank you for your help and your advice that rotation." Eric ran his hands over his head in the Martian gesture of respect. "I owe you."

Coni opened her mouth.

"Kid!" A commanding male voice echoed across the bar, before ringing out with laughter.

Eric jerked his arm out of the way as someone pushed past him.

A Terran boy, no older than six or seven, climbed onto Hawke's lap. She uncrossed her arms to give him space as he settled, showing her a handheld device.

"What did you fix?" Hawke asked.

"Chipreader." The boy rubbed some mechanical grease across his cheek as he replied.

She looked at the device again before moving her attention past Eric to an approaching Terran.

"See, Dent, fuckin useful." She ruffled the boy's brown hair, ignoring his protest as he pushed her hand away and climbed down. "Now, you can pay me what you owe me."

"Yeah, yeah, Nina." The man looked up at Eric. The slightly flattened nose of a break never mended properly cast a shadow over a wide mouth and angled jaw. "A Martian, out here?" His light blue, almost white eyes focused on Eric, and he ran a hand through his pale-yellow hair.

"Jon, this is Captain Jake Denthar." Kei motioned to the man. "Did not know you were back in port, Captain."

"By that, I assume you mean you didn't know my navigator was in port." Denthar laughed as Kei shrugged her shoulders in a noncommittal manner. Denthar extended his hand to Eric, who took it.

"Captain." Eric made a show of glancing up at the datascreens.

Denthar laughed again. "Not in the big leagues yet." He turned to Chris. "Number 16, 15?"

"12 on the UTC, Captain." Chris supplied.

Denthar shrugged at Eric.

"I always forget how tall they breed your lot." Denthar stepped back a little. "What brings you out to The Rim?"

"Not everyone enjoys fuckin history lessons, Dent."

Eric glanced at Hawke, catching the dark smile as Denthar rolled his eyes at her.

"You two will get along fine, then."

She shrugged, finishing her drink and putting the tumbler down.

"I need to get back to work." Eric was suddenly aware of the food-stained apron he was wearing amongst the company of those who might see nothing but credits if they looked hard enough at his skin colour or tattoos.

Hawke watched him as he rubbed a hand against the cloth. He motioned to Coni. "Thanks again."

She purred and nodded at him.

"Captains." He inclined his head at them both and Chris.

Kei smiled at those around the table, nodding. As she and Eric headed back towards the bar, her hand rested on his forearm.

"What?" Eric asked.

"You did well… Not everyone gets that kind of greeting."

Eric rubbed at his stiff shoulder, the result of constantly leaning over his workbench taking hold.

"What, you mean being assessed as if I am something to hunt?" he muttered at her, not wanting to be overheard, but smiled to soften his words. "And, found not worth it?"

"I guess." Kei giggled, showing her relief. "You also helped Coni out. She is protective of her crew. You won a few creds with that."

Eric mulled over the obvious game she had been playing with the bar. "At least you know someone's intentions when they point a gun in your direction."

"That is an interesting comment coming from a cook," said a male voice.

Eric froze mid-step. Kei's hand tightened on his forearm. Pointed at his face was the barrel of a handgun.

A rush of adrenaline overrode Eric's initial surge of fear. He recognised the man from the gaming table he had served earlier. He slowly raised his hands, focusing on the solid red ready light on the gun's barrel.

"My friend and I have a little disagreement." The man's tone matched the nasty twist to his smile.

There was a clunk of metal as the cyborg appeared near Eric's shoulder, the rifle in his hands held ready but not aimed.

"He seems to think—"

The air moved. Energy bullets cut the man off.

Grabbing Kei, Eric dropped, rolling them out of the way. Looking up at the crunch of metal, he saw Hawke break the cyborg's neck with one hard yank of her arm while she continued to fire into the chest of the armed man. His corpse crashed to the floor loudly, the gun in his hand clanging as it bounced away from Eric's reach.

"Mr Eric Hillar." Hawke said.

Smoke rose from the corpse's blackened clothes. The smell of cooked meat spread quickly in the air. The cyborg's body crashed to the floor. The loud sound ringing in Eric's ears.

She fired the gun into the back of the cyborg's neck, hitting its communication jacks. Taking a step forward, Hawke looked down at Eric and Kei. Smoke from several energy bullets fizzled out from the back of her jacket.

"You have a choice to make. Fuckin make it."

Hawke leapt away and somersaulted on her shoulder, avoiding more energy bullets. As she stood, she drew her second gun and started firing into the mezzanines.

Several emotions and thoughts flooded Eric. He looked at the doors to the kitchen, then down at Kei. She watched him silently.

There was sharp laughter from Hawke as she dodged bullets and returned fire. In the chaos, people ducked or dodged out from under the mezzanines.

Eric rose to his knees, looking around the bar, while Kei got into a crouch beside him. They watched the gunfight move about the room. Hawke never stood still long enough for anyone to get a shot in.

Behind him was that feeling of movement again. Eric remembered there were four at the gaming table just before the dull thunk of glass on the back of his head rattled him. The pain became sharp as the bottle broke. The tinkering sound of glass on the metal floor preceded a sticky, thick liquid pouring over his head, then down his neck and shoulders. It's sweet alcoholic smell was overpowering.

Anger surged as Eric spun on his knee and stood to face his attacker. His fist clipped the woman under her chin. There was a satisfying crunch of breaking bone as her head flew back at an odd angle and her body slammed into the metal panelling of the bar.

Eric tugged at his apron, tearing the straps off and dropped it to the ground. He glanced down at the crumpled uniform.

Kei, still in a crouch, looked up at him.

"Hide."

"Ok... Eric." She scrambled up and over the bar, dropping behind it as several bullets left black marks on the metal.

The sound of his name in Kei's cutting tone froze him for a second.

Two energy bullets hit his back. The icy burn from the stun spread quickly across his muscles. At the deep laughter, Eric turned again. He saw Denthar leaning against the table, watching.

Denthar rolled his eyes and motioned to Eric to duck.

Eric paused, realising he could no longer see the Kats and the boy at their table.

Three more bullets hit Eric's chest, forcing him back down to a knee. He followed their direction and saw someone near the mezzanine stairs. His vision blurred, the stun bullets taking effect on his nervous system, and the shooter disappeared from his sight. The cold spread across his body, making his muscles weak and his reactions painfully slow.

Shaking his head, trying to clear it of the fog, he looked up, seeing Hawke land on someone a few metres away. Her feet planted squarely on their chest, she fired into their face. More bullets hit her jacket, fizzling out with a static charge on its armour.

Eric fumbled as he tried to stand. His balance was gone, his limbs refusing to obey. He dropped a hand to the floor to steady himself. Eric cradled his head with his other. His focus faded in and out.

A pair of boots moved into his line of vision, before hearing the hum of an active gun.

"Five stun bullets and you are still conscious." There was a note of appreciation in their voice.

Eric recognised the last of the Terrans from the poker table. Their nose was pierced with a bullring made of crystal. It cast a bright rainbow of light around the bar as they moved. Several beams blinded Eric's vision, sending stabs of pain across his temple.

"At least I do not need to share the bounty, thanks to you and her." The speaker glanced at Hawke.

Eric threw himself back out of the gun's aim and swept his arm across, the force knocking his opponent's legs from under them. They hit the ground with a thump.

Eric reversed his swing and brought his hand down hard on his attacker's neck. Bones crushed under the impact. Eric watched them choke a few times before the foam on their lips stilled.

He tried to stand again but his legs could not take his weight. He struggled for a few moments, but the stun shots had finally numbed his legs and all they could do was twitch.

Kei crouched behind him, her hand on his shoulder.

"You need to move." She looked up as a shadow approached them.

"You're fuckin meant to drink that. Not wear it." Hawke crouched in front of them.

Eric blinked, trying to focus on the captain.

She holstered her guns. Her expression was one of disgust.

"Fuckin waste." Her boots crunched on the shattered glass and sticky floor surrounding him.

"Tell… that… to them." His tongue felt thick, like he had drunk too much rum.

Kei's hand on his shoulder tightened.

Hawke snorted, looking at the corpses surrounding them. She turned back to Eric and, with a quick movement, grabbed his wrist and dragged him up.

Eric tried to look for Kei as her hand fell from his shoulder.

Hawke's nose wrinkled as she sniffed the alcohol covering him. "Probably a better use for it." She hooked his arm over her shoulder and lifted him again. "Stuff tastes as bad as it smells. It's fuckin shit."

"Mars." Eric slurred, trying to move, but his legs still refused to obey him.

Hawke's grip on his wrist tightened enough to be painful through the fog.

"How strong are you?"

She dragged him along as she headed towards a glass wall.

"You always have to go for the fight." Amusement saturated Denthar's voice.

Eric turned to look in his direction, but his head drooped forward. He managed a few faltering steps as he tried to keep up with Hawke, but it only increased the fog.

"Just get your crew ready, Dent."

Eric's thoughts trailed away, forming only half questions before disappearing as she carried him out the black doors.

The metal grillwork of Sirius's floors rolled up and down in his sight. His feet fell behind.

Hawke grabbed his belt and lifted him higher, almost over her shoulder.

Rough fingers pulled the translator from his ear. Eric heard Hawke spit some command he did not understand. There was a blur of red and tan as she shoved something into his ear to replace it.

He fell sharply and hard onto the firm padding of a landsled's seat.

The device in his ear beeped. A pair of soft padded hands checked the back of his skull.

"Don't let the fucker puke everywhere."

Eric gave into the darkness.

The distinct smell of medical alcohol made Eric's nose twitch. He groaned from the pain in the back of his head, its low thump pulsing in his ears. Above him, the stark lights and white ceiling swirled in his vision.

"Be careful." A soft purr accompanied Coni's voice. "Do not move too quickly."

He blinked as her words sunk into his conscious but took a moment to understand. Rubbing at the grime in his eyes, moving the sweat that caked them shut, Eric rolled his head on the pillow towards her.

She smiled and leaned over to check the back of his skull with her soft, padded fingers again. "Just a nasty bump. It will feel better in a few hours."

"It's the thick fuckin skull." Hawke's tone was scathing.

Eric looked past Coni and focused on the captain, seeing that callous smile again. She leaned against the meditable. Her jacket now gone. A sleeveless top exposed her arms that were crossed at her chest. Her stylised feather tattoos started at her neck and went down to her wrist on one arm and to her palm on the other. They twisted and turned, their black lines only occasionally broken from scars that were even whiter than her skin.

She stared back at him.

"What the fuck made you think you could hide in plain fuckin sight?"

"Hide in…" Eric sat up slowly, careful not to send his head spinning again.

Coni watched him. Her ears turned towards Hawke, whiskers twitching.

"For fuck's sake." Hawke expelled a frustrated breath and she glared at the ceiling. A long moment later, she lowered her gaze to stare at him again. "You didn't think some fucker was goin to recognise your skin, or those fuckin tattoos?"

Eric touched his forehead, running his hand over his skull and across his tattoos. He winced, triggering a wave of throbbing pain.

As Hawke breathed, the ink covering her own skin moved.

"And you?" Eric countered, his brain scrambling for time to orientate itself.

Coni's ears pressed against her skull as Hawke laughed.

"I'm not hidin." She looked at her arm and appeared to consider her tattoos for a moment, before dropping her hand to her holsters and drawing a gun. With a smooth, well-practised motion, she raised it and flicked the safety off. The barrel pointed at the ceiling as the safety light went from green to red. The battery lit up the gun's charge indicator: *red, orange, yellow,* then *green.*

"And most idiots have enough brains not to bother tryin for my bounty."

"Looked to me like there were a few guns aimed at you." Eric pinched his nose, trying to remember the fight and the details at the edges of his vision. He looked up to see the captain shrug and holster the gun.

"There's always a few that'll try their hand."

Coni stood straighter, her ears unfolding.

Hawke crossed her arms again. "You're just fuckin lucky they had their guns on stun."

"My insides do not feel that way," Eric muttered.

"Then maybe you shouldn't have been playin fuckin house as a cook." Her words dripped with contempt.

"Captain." Coni's protest was quiet but Hawke heard her.

With a roll of her eyes, she straightened. "If I didn't fuckin need him, I'd have fuckin shot him myself, Con."

Hawke turned back to Eric as he blinked, reacting to her words with a small jerk of surprise.

"Yes, need. You've a rep for brains accordin to the FIS files. Was wonderin if that was a farce too. I'll give you a cluey and you've got a chance to prove those brains."

"Debatable, Captain." Eric sighed, massaging the back of his neck. A chill ran down his spine at the mention of Fleet Internal Security. "Figured here was good for a fresh start, but…"

Hawke's snort sounded more amused than derogatory.

"Fresh start, yes." Coni smiled and Eric registered a vibration in the surrounding air. Her purring soothed the headache. "But not when there is a bounty of ten thousand trade credits on your skin. Skin that stands out so easily here."

"You knew?"

"Wolf saw you arrivin." Hawke patted the table she was leaning against. Her voice had lost that sharp edge, the smile returning.

Eric straightened his shoulders and looked around. He noted the medical equipment, including the two meditables—the one he was on, the other Hawke was leaning against. He saw storage cabinets and a sink at the back of the space, plus the two shut doors.

"So, this is the inside of a pirate ship," Eric mused. "And not just any. The Werewolf. Did not imagine ever ending up here. Breathing, that is." He could not stop the tone of disappointment in his words. "Looks just like any other ship. What is her secret?"

Coni laughed.

"We can allow that they've given you a fuckin education."

His shoulders shook with silent laughter.

Hawke raised her eyebrows. "At least I amuse someone."

"Captain." Coni's purr intensified as Eric looked back at Hawke.

"You can thank Kei." He confessed. "And three cycles listening to the chatter in Rebeal's commonroom."

Hawke flicked a hand in a dismissive motion.

"Wastin time." She stood and pointed at his ear. "Now, tell her I haven't eaten you—yet—or I really will do something rash." She started for the door. "When you're finished, we gotta have words. Words about your future and exactly how fuckin long it may be." She looked at Coni. "Show him to the bridge when it's done."

They watched the door shut behind her.

"And that is Captain Hawke." Coni's purr settled into a low rumble, tail swinging gently. After a few quick breaths, her fur flattened and her shoulders dropped as they relaxed.

Eric exhaled.

"She is always rough before a job. And, when dealing with strangers." She blinked, rotating her shoulders as tension left her stance. "But she is not lying. We need you for this one." Coni saw the doubt in his expression. "Ok… She and Captain Denthar know they need someone like you for this job."

"After all I have heard, I expected more anger and violence."

Coni stared at him. Her expression unreadable for a minute. "Oh, she gets angry. Trust me on that."

"Did not see this coming when I got up for my shift." Eric rubbed at the back of his head again, wincing at the pain from the increased pressure.

Coni chirruped, her mouth opening in a fang-filled smile.

"Captain has opened you a line to Kei." Her tail flicked behind her again. "I will take you to the bridge when you are ready." She walked out the door, leaving Eric alone.

He reached for the commlink device in his ear. It felt smaller and more streamlined compared to his old model translator. He tapped the button on it and waited for the device to ping a start-up sequence.

"Kei?"

Kei said, <Is it Jon or Eric?>

He winced at her dark tone. He had heard her angry before but never directly at him.

"Sorry, Kei." Hearing her voice, Eric realised that he desperately wanted her to understand. He looked at the ceiling, bringing her face to his thoughts. "It was easier to hide if no one knew."

Kei, <I know.>

Eric's eyes narrowed as the anger left her voice quickly.

Kei, <I have just been worried. Nothing for over half a rotation. Sasha is not happy.>

Eric shifted on the table and leaned back against the wall, his eyes closed. His legs dangled off the edge as he settled.

Kei, <Eric?>

He smiled.

"Say that again."

Kei, <What, that Sasha is—>

"No." Eric cut her off. "My name."

Kei, <Eric?>

His smile got a little wider.

Kei, <Seriously? That is all you can say? Hawke is dangerous.>

"She does not seem that bad."

Kei inhaled sharply.

Eric laughed. "Besides, she will not shoot me if I am useful to her."

Kei, <Just so long as you stay useful.>

"Yeah." Eric crossed his arms, getting comfortable. "Tell Sasha I am sorry. I really tried to stay out of trouble." He sighed. "I never could, you know."

Kei, <You should have stayed in the kitchen.> There was a hint of amusement in her voice and Eric laughed.

#

Eric stepped through the airlock into the bridge and stopped. Stars glowed brilliantly against the black blue of space. All the colours of the spectrum seemed to be there as he stared at the wondrous sight. The windowscreen was empty of datawindows, leaving the image of the stars and Sirius unbroken. In contrast to the colour, hundreds of metal ships orbited the spacestation.

Occasionally, a small burst of energy from a booster flickered in the dirty greys, keeping the ships in their orbits. Mostly hidden by the bulk of Sirius was the tiny white dwarf sun it anchored nearby.

"Better fuckin lookin on the outside." Hawke's dry tone directed Eric's attention to where she sat at the front of the bridge. She appeared to be staring at the stars but in the windowscreen's reflection, she looked directly at him.

The boy was sitting on her lap, his legs dangling. He turned to watch Eric over her shoulder, his green eyes bright.

Werewolf's bridge was a basic two-by-two configuration. A single central walkway passed each pair and ended at the console that ran the width of the room and the windowscreen above it. The high-backed chairs were covered in dark woven cloth and turned at multiple angles to their consoles or the centre walkway. Around the space, lights blinked and screens ran code.

"Never quite seen it like this," Eric admitted, walking towards the front of the bridge. His eyes stayed on the expanse of space in front of the ship. Stopping as he reached the front chairs, he glanced at Hawke, their eyes meeting in the windowscreen's reflection again.

"Kid, go tell Chris to quit gamin and show you that program he's supposed to be fuckin runnin on the mainframe. Now."

The boy climbed down slowly and shuffled past Eric silently before bolting out of the bridge.

Eric looked back at Hawke in time to catch a glimmer of silver in her eyes. She had turned the seat to watch him, her arms crossed. He shivered, uncomfortable at her intensive gaze. The reaction surprised him and he refocused on her face.

It was then he noticed her irises were larger than a Terrans'. They covered most of the surface of her eyes, eliminating most of the white you would normally see. The gold colour was reflective, showing the lights of the stars across their surface.

"Sit the fuck down." Hawke spoke slowly, carefully.

Eric heard the impatience, but she had it mostly under control. He sat in the copilot seat, forcing his gaze to stay on her and not return to the windowscreen.

"You killed those hunters."

He nodded, mentally adding two more to his growing list. Eric rubbed at the back of his neck, her gaze making his skin prickle with unease. He felt like there was a target marked between his shoulder blades, even though she was sitting in front of him.

"And Sasha has her fuckin rules."

"Yeah."

Hawke expelled her breath and looked at the ceiling for a long moment. "I'm not fuckin used to bein the instigator of conversation." She drew another breath and returned her gaze to him.

Eric smiled as he breathed deep, trying to settle the sudden nerves. "I am a bit out of my depth here… Captain."

Using her title had a mild calming effect on her. Hawke's arms unfolded and lowered to the armrest of her seat as she rolled her eyes.

"Typical fuckin Martian… Honest."

"You could say I am a product of my upbringing." Eric relaxed a little as her mouth curved into a tight smile.

She glanced at a datascreen in her console, then at the scene of ships in the windowscreen.

"Finally, someone with a fuckin sense of humour," she muttered quietly.

Unsure if he should have heard, Eric kept his mouth shut.

The stars returned to her eyes as she looked back at him.

"A convoy is comin close enough to be worth it. It's got supplies you know very well. And you're gonna help us steal them."

Eric tensed. "I would not say I know much of anything… Unless you are counting mining gear?"

That cold, predatory smile appeared.

"You are kidding?"

"Nope." Her expression sent an icy shiver down his spine. "We can steal the parts but can't fuckin recognise if they've been tampered with."

"I see." Eric looked at the windowscreen, swallowing to regain moisture in his mouth. "And what if I really know nothing about mining and I really was a simple cook back on Mars?"

"Smarter than pretendin to know and failin me." She looked at the window again. "Bit different from the view of a cargohold."

Eric heard her move the pilot chair, followed by a clunk as she dumped her boots on the navigational computer between the seats.

"And, lucky for you, I know you're fuckin lyin about that cook nonsense."

Eric turned to respond but stopped. Her expression was calm, almost peaceful.

"This view isn't the only perk either."

"Perk?" Eric was sure he saw light glint off her teeth.

"Pirates get paid." She shrugged and gave him that nasty smile. "We get paid a fuck load better than a cook."

They turned to the windowscreen as a ship pulled up in front of them, facing Werewolf. Several hundred metres long, the ship was thin and streamlined. The three main engines set in the standard Terran triangle at her rear, clustered close together. Extra booster jets littered the rest of the hull. Eric noted the obvious armaments across its reinforced hull as the running lights from Sirius created a pattern of yellow and blue across its metal.

Denthar said, <Well, Nina. I hope this is worth denyin the crew their shore leave.>

Hawke rolled her eyes and tapped her commlink.

"Fuck, Dent. You'd think this was Xenoxal."

Denthar, <I got debtors to pay.>

"Yeah, me." She turned back to Eric. "Well, Mr Hillar?"

"You said yes," Chris observed from his seat. The cyborg looked up from the mainframe and the boy next to him. The dry metallic edge to his voice cut through Eric's thoughts.

Eric shrugged. Stepping off the stairs, he stopped on the commonroom grillwork next to a large table. "Saw little choice."

The boy turned, saw Eric, and bolted back up the stairs.

"Weird kid."

The mainframe took up half the length of the wall to Eric's right. Its consoles and several chairs, like those on the bridge, took up most of this space. Next to him, a large ten-seater table sat in the middle of the room, cutting the space in half, its chairs strewn around it. Hawke's jacket hung on the back of one. In front of that chair, on the table, was a half empty bottle of whiskey and four tumblers. On the other side of the table, at the edge of the mainframe, a second set of stairs led down to the lower level.

A couch took up most of the rest of the room. Coni lounged on it, a large datascreen facing her. On the back wall were a set of closed double airlock doors. To Eric's left there was another single airlock.

Coni looked up from the datapad she was reading. "We all get some choice." She smiled.

Eric rubbed the nagging sore spot on his head. "I did not see any."

Coni frowned. "Captain stuck her neck out for you," she chirruped and started purring. "Stopping Grong's hunters and all."

"Funny, I thought she was looking for a fight myself." Eric realised he was rubbing at the scar on his wrist. He pulled his hands apart, watching the Kats as Chris turned to his sister, a smile on his face revealed metal fangs. "Now what?"

Chris turned back to the mainframe as they heard the engines rumble. "Two sequences to the rendezvous."

Chris picked up some datacables laying on the console, their wires looped around on the dataentry keys. They connected to some plugs in the panelling below. He started plugging them into the jacks on the back of his neck.

"We wait." The Kat sat back in his chair. His eyes filled with datalines as he connected to the mainframe. "I need to finish these systems checks."

Eric looked down at his dirty clothes. Blood, alcohol and dirt stained the white top and black pants of the Rebeal kitchen outfit. "Got anywhere I can clean up? Or some clean clothes, at least?"

Coni chirruped again and stood, pointing to the floor near him. Eric followed her directions and saw his backpack dumped against the leg of a chair. Over it was his jacket.

"You guys work fast," he observed, moving towards his things. She shrugged as he hooked the backpack over his arm and picked up his jacket.

"You were out for a few hours." Coni jumped over the couch and stopped near the stairwell by the mainframe, motioning for him to follow her. "Although for a while there, I thought Kei was going to refuse to hand your belongings over."

"You know Kei?" Eric joined her and followed her down the stairs.

"Last longer than a few cycles in Rebeal, most people get to know you." Coni inclined her head, her ears slightly folded.

He glanced down at her, eyes narrowing as he heard the neutral, rehearsed tone in her voice.

"Surprised they did not recognise you until now."

"I got comfortable." Eric sighed. "Should have stayed in the kitchen if I was going to stay unnoticed. Only got me to blame there."

"True." Coni waited for him at the bottom of the stairs. "Surprised you see that."

"I learned a long time ago that if I did not recognise my mistakes, I would die from them."

"Do all Martians think like you?" Coni's ears faced forward towards Eric. Her irises dilated and focused on his face.

He considered the question for a moment. His boots stopped on the grillwork of the corridor. He took in the rows of closed airlocks running along both sides. Four evenly spaced ones on the left and seven on the right. He could see the stairwell they had used to go up to the bridge at the ship's front end. The other side of the corridor ended in another set of double airlock doors.

"I guess." He smiled. "I figure when you grow up on a UTC-controlled planet, you either let others do the thinking for you or you learn to be introspective."

Coni's tail flicked, her stance straightening. She pointed to two doors on the left side of the wall, heading towards the back of the ship. "Ok, this side: Captain's quarters and gym." She then pointed to the first two doors on the left wall, directly in front of them. "You have seen the medibay, and that's the galley."

She motioned at the doors on the right, at the rear of the ship. "Empty, Angel's, empty, Chris's." She used a pair of fingers to point at the two doors for Chris. "Mine and empty." She turned back to him. "Take your pick."

"Angel?" Eric blinked. "The boy?"

She nodded.

"How did he end up here?"

"Captain found him on a spacestation. Not sure of the specifics. Before our time on Wolf." She shrugged. "She took a shine to him."

"Never thought I would find a boy on a ship like this." Eric moved down the corridor.

He paused at the galley, looking in as curiosity got the better of him. About the same size as the medibay, it had one door on the far wall and another to his right. Marked with symbols for cold storage, the door in the rear was closed. The other was open, revealing an overgrown greenroom. The rest of the space was full of cabinets and cooking equipment.

"Actually, not that uncommon." Coni joined him and smiled, noticing what he was looking at. "Help yourself to the galley. It is open to anyone. Gym is the captain's. You will hear her in there at some point. It sounds like she's making a mess of someone but it is just the practice dummy."

"Thought she was more the guns type." He turned and looked at the closed door opposite them. "Also figure the rooms are all the same?" She nodded as he opened it.

The room was bigger than the one he had shared with Kei. A large bed sat against the right wall, while a standard desk was to his left. A walled off wetspace at the back filled most of the room. He dumped the backpack and jacket on the bed and looked around.

"A hydroshower?"

"Wolf's tanks can handle it," Coni replied from the doorway.

"And a greenroom?"

She smiled in answer.

"Being a pirate has its perks." Eric smiled, repeating Hawke's line.

Coni purred.

"What do you mean it is not uncommon to have kids out on these ships?"

"Think about it." Coni smiled and tapped some commands into the control panel near the door. "If you are a wanted criminal, where is the safest place to put the ones you care about? Right next to you where they cannot be taken hostage or arrested." She checked the information on the display. "Your space now. You can put in a code to lock the door. Also, you can take your commlink off in here but do not leave the room without it on. Werewolf has internal security. If she does not recognise you, you will meet the nasty end of it."

Eric laughed. "Now that sounds like the paranoid Hawke I have heard about."

Coni smiled. She headed away from the doorway. "Get cleaned up and settle in. We will be in the commonroom when you finish."

Eric waited until the door shut before moving to his backpack. His clothes were neat and placed inside it carefully. As he pulled a few out, the handgun rolled out of the cloth and thumped onto the bed. He stared at it for a moment, remembering those first few hours on Sirius. It had been cycles since he had hidden it in the room he shared with Kei. He had almost forgotten about it.

#

Feeling refreshed after the long shower and his headache now almost gone, Eric found his way into the greenroom. Dressed in a pair of deep brown pants and a white t-shirt—which he owned multiples of—he felt like Eric again. The idea of Jon the Cook faded fast from his mind.

He crouched under a large protein plant to look at a small bush with bright yellow and red tubers.

"End of fuckin discussion, Con."

Hawke's voice raised as he heard steps into the galley behind him. Turning, he watched as she passed the open door.

Coni stopped at the entrance to the galley. Her fur standing up and her ears low.

"But, Captain, I thought this was a basic trader convoy, not a UTC—"

"What part of 'pirate' is hard to fuckin understand?" Hawke's voice deepened into that scathing tone Eric heard earlier. "They've the best gear. Dent's got the crew to get it done fast and, if I'm lucky, I'll get to shoot a few FPs. And, if I'm really fuckin lucky, they'll have an FIS or two."

"But the UTC again? They will not take it lightly, Captain."

There was a noise of someone rummaging through a draw.

Hawke snorted. When she spoke again, her tone was not as angry. "Is that all you're worried about?"

Coni's ears straightened and her fur flattened. "If your bounty gets any higher, those like Grong will start paying attention."

Eric saw the deep breath the Kat took, her shoulders losing some of their tension.

"You know he focuses on UTC bounties."

"It makes the downtime more interestin. Besides, it's about time Grong and I had some words about his hunters and their limits." Hawke snorted. "It's fuckin inevitable. Those dicks in Rebeal were his. He'll come at me now, even if it's just for fuckin appearances."

"Is that all you care about? Making number one on the MWLs? What happens when they tag you as wanted dead?" Coni sighed and rolled her eyes. "Sticks'n'cubes? Captain, you need to eat more than that."

"Don't you fuckin start." Hawke passed back across the doorway. "Let's face it, Con, if we don't have a goal, what's the point?" Her voice faded as her footsteps went up the nearby stairs.

Eric reached the doorway.

Coni turned to the sound. She had tucked her tail against a leg but her fur smoothed out and she smiled at him.

"UTC convoy?"

She nodded in answer.

He angled his head as he thought aloud. "You know, they have the best mining gear. It is Martian-designed, after all."

"Already thinking like a pirate?" She smiled to soften the comment as they followed Hawke up the stairs.

"Just stating fact."

They reached the commonroom. Hawke was pouring herself a drink. Angel sat next to her, playing with some circuit boards and chewing on a protein stick from the open bag on the table.

"Truth is, if word gets out what we are going for... cargo gets extra security." Coni found a chair at the table, motioning for Eric to join her.

Hawke watched them as he sat a few chairs from her.

"All in one approach?" Eric waited for the confirming nod from Coni. "Yeah, UTC agents are clever. Sometimes, that is the best option. Did it myself a few times on Mars."

"You will have to tell us about it one rotation."

"Not much to it, really." Eric sighed, leaning back in his chair, the memories weighing heavily on his chest. "Did not want to get involved. I had just lost one daughter and was trying to keep the other out of the troubles. Simply in the wrong place at the wrong time."

"Or right time." Hawke watched him as she drank.

Eric felt like he was being assessed again.

"Grong's hunters, Varsely's dicks in that ambush. You've a knack for killin."

Coni shook her head at Hawke. "Captain has her own spin on the universe."

"We're not in one of your fuckin happy ever after tales, Con."

"One rotation, Captain," Coni shot back, "you are going to meet someone, and you are going to realise there is more to life."

Eric realised he was seeing a continuing conversation from a previous time.

Hawke finished her drink. As she lowered the empty tumbler to the table, the dark, edgy smile Hawke gave Coni chilled him.

"Trust me." Her voice froze the air in the room. "You never want me meetin the one that can stand by my side."

Coni sat back, considering Hawke's words.

Eric watched Coni's ears turn and her tail did a lazy loop. The look she gave Hawke was strange to him. He could only think of it as pity, and the thought of pitying Captain Hawke was alien.

"You have a sad view of the stars, Captain."

Hawke shrugged, pouring another drink. "Whole place is full of fuckin Terrans." She twirled the bottle lid on and lifted her glass, swirling the whiskey in it. "It'll probably be better to burn it all fuckin down instead."

"Virus." Angel mumbled around his protein stick.

Coni looked at the boy, her ears drooping. "Do you have to teach him that?" Her purr turned uneven.

Hawke laughed quietly as she leaned over to ruffle his hair. He protested, pushing her hand away.

"Virus?" Eric sat up, looking at them.

"Terrans are a fuckin virus." Hawke tipped her glass towards Eric before taking another drink.

"They spread out, consume resources, kill, or assimilate everything in their path. Virus." Angel grinned.

Eric blinked as he realised it was the boy who had spoken. "How old are you?"

"Six."

The boy's grin got bigger, showing sharp teeth. Eric paled. Hawke shrugged as he looked at her for confirmation.

"And what does that make you, Captain?" Coni countered.

"Never said I was any fuckin better."

Eric caught the glint again as she drank, confirming her own set of sharp teeth. He sat back while Coni shook her head. He looked back at the boy.

"Well." He breathed, trying to shake the chilling feeling. "This virus might as well keep busy whilst here. What do you like to eat?"

"Coolios." The boy's green eyes focused on Eric.

Hawke snorted as she drank her whiskey, half coughing, half laughing. She rested the tumbler on the table whilst she cleared her throat.

"Greasy burgers from a food vendor on Sirius." Coni explained, smiling at Hawke. "Captain is rather partial to them too."

"Just make sure it's got fuckin meat in it." Hawke stood. "There's plenty of it in storage."

Angel watched her leave, then turned back to him. "Burger?"

"Ok, let us see how I stack up to Coolios."

Eric placed the plate in front of Angel. The boy looked at the burger suspiciously. Chris and Coni joined them at the table, taking their plates off Eric before sitting. Sliding the last two onto the table's surface, Eric found a chair. Hawke did not leave the mainframe. She leaned over one of the control panels, looking inside its open casing.

"Go on, try it." Eric urged the crew.

Chris picked his burger up and took a big bite, while Coni nibbled at hers.

The boy looked up at Eric, then back to the burger. He took the bun off the top, looked at the contents, then turned towards Hawke, who was now watching them. Eric noticed her tiny nod to the boy before he refocused on the plate and the burger.

Eric opened his mouth to protest as Angel pulled the greens and tomato out, before squishing the top bun back on and biting into it.

Hawke laughed.

Angel nodded at Eric, making enjoyment noises through his mouthful.

"It tastes better with all of it." Eric looked at the food Angel had left on the plate.

"Captain, can we keep him?" Chris devoured half of his burger already. "Actual food."

Eric looked at Hawke, who continued to watch them with crossed arms, her expression unchanged, then to Chris, who ate with enthusiasm.

"Do you have a holster for that handgun?"

Eric met her eyes for a moment. Now that he had noticed their strangeness, he could not match her stare for long. He ducked his head to his plate, picking up his own burger.

"No." He took a bite. The food tasted sour in his mouth. He mentally reviewed his bag. He had noticed no tampering when he had unpacked.

Hawke had not moved when he looked up again.

"When you're finished, bring it to the hangar." She turned and left through the far airlock.

Eric caught a view of the darkness beyond the door before it shut.

"Hangar?" He glanced between the Kats as they shared a look.

"That was different." Chris turned back to his burger. "Normally, she takes a while to get used to someone new on Wolf. What was it with us?" He looked at his sister.

"Couple of cycles." Coni had a thoughtful expression as she stared at the closed airlock. "She is territorial." Coni looked at Eric, recovering her tone and voice. "Does not like changes in her space."

"I am not really a change, am I?" Eric countered. "Only here for the job."

"True." Chris turned to Angel. "What do you think, kid? Better than Coolios?"

"Needs more meat." Angel did not let the criticism stop him from finishing his burger.

The boy stood on his chair, reaching over the table for the last plate and pulled it towards himself. Repeating the move, he took the fresh food out of the burger and left the patty. He crammed the bun back down with the palm of his hand, picked up the burger and took a large bite.

"But good." He managed around a mouthful.

Eric sighed as the Kats laughed.

#

Following Coni's directions, Eric headed down the corridor from his room to the rear of the ship. The reinforced airlock opened into a dark and empty cargobay. As he stepped through it, two sentry guns unfolded from above the door, their indicator lights blinking red as they aimed at him. His commlink beeped and their lights turned to green before folding back into their storage compartments.

The doors behind Eric closed. His dark vision kicked in and he let out a breath.

He was standing on a catwalk on the second level of a three-storey space. One level below him, he could see the grillwork and cargobay doors. There was a ladder in front of him attached to the handrail. It went down to the lower floor and up to a third level catwalk above. The other side of the cargobay had three single storey airlocks. He headed towards the one on his level.

As Eric moved along the catwalk, he passed the floor-to-ceiling airlock on the right side of the cargobay. He glanced at the mirrored door on the other side of the bay. It took a moment for him to realise that the catwalk he was on retracted on itself, allowing for larger goods to be moved between the cargobays. Eric wondered if they had ever stolen something that needed such a large opening to fit through.

He stopped as he reached the door and looked up into the shadows of the ceiling. He could see the form of an industrial crane, and tracks that went in the directions of the side and back doors.

Behind him, the airlock opened. Eric spun, raising his gun. He blinked as the lights from the next room briefly blinded him. He shook his shoulders from the tension and breathed as his sight readjusted. The gun lowered back to his side and he stepped through the airlock.

Hawke had refitted the cargobay behind it into a hangar and had filled the space with gear and supplies to keep several smaller transports in operation. A couple of workbenches sat at the side of the doors.

On the other side of the bay was a six-bay transport rack. Along the bottom row were a pair of two-person bombers and a light transport ship. On the upper-level, Eric recognised the shape of a single-person UTC fighter wrapped in storage cloth.

Near them, some mechanical arms were holding a familiar looking red and tan landsled off the grillwork. Hawke was underneath it, working on something.

Eric stepped into the room, closer to her.

"Why am I not surprised that sled is yours?"

The sensors on the airlocks closed the doors behind him.

Hawke paused and looked at him from the shadows. She climbed out from under the sled and dusted her arms.

Eric saw the age of the landsled with its dents and scratches along its faded paint.

"The fighter?" Eric glanced at it in its wrappings.

"None of your fuckin business." The order was explicit in her tone as she went to the workbench behind them and poured herself a whiskey.

Eric smiled as she put the bottle down and lifted the tumbler. "How many of those do you have stashed around the ship?"

Hawke looked at the glass and shrugged. "Probably not enough."

She leaned against the table and pointed to a crate a few metres from them. "There."

Following her direction, Eric looked inside the crate to find a pile of guns, holsters, spare batteries and even some flash grenades. He tested a few types of holsters: a thigh holster like Hawke's, a hip holster and, finally, a side holster. The heavy handgun felt odd against his ribs, but the draw was the most comfortable of the three. He adjusted the straps around his shoulders and back as he turned to Hawke. She was studying him again. He went cold, shivering, under the intense gaze.

"Your file doesn't say how a miner became the first terrorist in 2000 revolutions."

"And one of the Rebeal commonroom's favourite drinking games is trying to figure out where you come from."

Hawke responded with a chuckle and a gulp of whiskey.

"Like I said, wrong place, wrong time."

"I take it you know how to use that?" She pointed at the gun with her glass.

Eric drew it and ran a finger down the barrel. "Point this end at the target."

"For fuck's sake." She let out a loud groan. She put the drink down and pushed past him to the crate. "You need to draw, fire and kill, and be faster than the fuck tryin to do the same to you."

She pulled out several batteries, shoving them into his hands and then pulled out a pair of strange guns. They looked like medical temperature readers and fit in her hands easily, with a short barrel and a small display that lit up as she flicked them on.

Eric noticed that glimmer in her eyes. He swallowed as the rim of the cargobay doors lit up with blue light. The solid doors opened to reveal multicoloured lines in the inky black of space.

Hawke snorted. "Good instincts at least."

Eric had stepped towards the control panel for the exterior doors, even as he realised that the blue light that ringed their frame was an electronic airlock. The air in the bay did not quiver. He watched the lines of light from the stars as they flew past Faster-Than-Light. He heard the distant sounds of engines rotating up in power.

"Transport would be useless if we couldn't get it outta Wolf."

"That's what FTL looks like?" Eric stared at the lines as they bent.

Hawke grunted and jumped forward. Rolling across the grillwork, she fired the guns into the space beyond the airlock. Even as she stood, she shot a few more times. Turning back to him, she passed him one gun.

Eric looked at the display. It showed five distance measurements in light years. He blinked and looked back at Hawke.

"Target practise? You shoot stars in FTL for target practise?"

"If you prefer to be dead, then by all fuckin means, skip the practise." She turned the other gun off and tossed it back into the crate. She frowned and looked up at him. "They grow your lot fuckin tall, don't they?"

"I guess." Eric fitted the gun into the palm of his hand and fired a test shot. The gun whined an error reading and reset. He tried again, wincing at the second error. "I am curious about one thing." Turning to speak to her, he noticed she was back at the workbench, glass in hand.

Hawke inclined her head for him to continue.

Turning back to the starlines, he aimed and fired again. "What did Xion do to justify that mess at Rebeal? No one seems to know." He turned back as she laughed. The sound was dark and bitter.

"Interested in keepin your skin on?"

"And understanding Captain Hawke a little better."

"He was FIS. FIS that was askin about a lone Martian." That dark edge returned to her smile as she spoke slowly. "I had a time dependant job and no time to deal with the inevitable fuckin mess. That, and he implied one too many times that he was the man to defrost this Ice Bitch."

"Fleet Internal Security? Out here?" Eric swallowed, his mouth suddenly dry.

"Got them all out on The Rim." Hawke pointed her glass at him. "Who told you to stop practisin?"

She waited until Eric had gone back to shooting before speaking again. "Werewolf."

"Sorry?" He looked back at her.

"You said people in Rebeal's commonroom wanted to know where I'm from." She finished the drink. "Tell them Wolf. It ain't no fuckin secret."

Eric found a slow smile forming as he tried his aim again. He cursed when the gun beeped in error a third time.

0.10

The starlines receded back into distant stars as Eric entered the bridge, his jacket over his shoulder. Chris and Coni were at their preferred stations in the middle row. Coni sat at the communications console, while Chris sat at the sensors chair. The back two seats for the ship's systems and weapons consoles were vacant.

Hawke sat in the pilot chair, Angel on her lap. He helped her fly with his hands over hers.

The tapping of Chris's steel claws was loud in the quiet. Coni had one fingerpad pressing her commlink into her ear as she looked at a datascreen near her.

"Denthar is not here yet." Coni fiddled with the frequencies. "No convoy either."

"Dent will be late to his own fuckin funeral," Hawke muttered. She tapped Angel on the shoulder and pointed at the copilot seat.

The boy looked up at her silently.

"Now."

Angel climbed down and slumped into the other chair.

Hawke looked at the reflection of the bridge and saw Eric. "Sit your arse down."

He glanced at his options and chose the weapons chair, turning it to watch the windowscreen.

"Space compression," Chris warned.

On the windowscreen, a blue box highlighted a section of space. That same ship from Sirius appeared for a few seconds before disappearing under a burst of light. Eric focused on the spot, seeing just the hint of a shimmer against the stars that was its cloaking shield.

"Dent. Thought you'd gotten lost." Hawke's tone had that hint of amusement.

Denthar, <You boosted Wolf's speed again.>

"You're gettin slow."

Denthar, <I hope our new friend survived his first trip with you?>

Eric turned to see Hawke staring at him in the windowscreen's reflection. She frowned when her gaze went to his holster and handgun.

"Still breathin." She turned to Chris. "Get him a rifle. His aim ain't worth a fuck with that thing."

Chris nodded and left the bridge.

Denthar, <You didn't force those star-cursed distance shooters on him?>

Eric smiled while Hawke did her customary stare at the ceiling for a few breaths.

Denthar, <You did, didn't you, Nina?>

"I want to be alive to spend my fuckin money," Hawke bit back. "I'll always enjoy your share if you blow out the side of the hull and you all fuckin die."

Denthar, <Who're you kiddin? You spend it all on that rust bucket anyway.>

The blue box became a red target marker. Hawke's sharp laughter filled the bridge as they heard panic on the other side of the comms.

Denthar, <How'd you do that?>

Eric glanced at the console as she turned off the targeting from the front of the bridge.

Denthar, <How can Wolf even see Charger?>

Chris returned, a pair of rifles slung over his shoulder by their straps and his own side holster dangling from his grip. He handed a rifle to Eric. The Kat strapped the gunbelt to his waist while he watched the datascreens on his console.

"I helped you outfit her... Or is your old age affectin the memory too, Dent?"

Eric tapped the rifle against his collarbone and tested the sight and the battery. Satisfied, he put the weapon down by his side and tested the reach of the handgun. Next, he tested the reach of the spare batteries that hung off the straps against his ribs.

Denthar, <Hilarious.>

Eric pulled his jacket on and tugged it into place, then slung the rifle over a shoulder.

"Interestin." Hawke was watching him when he looked up. "Looks like you might actually come in handy, Hillar."

"I should have grabbed a few grenades from that crate," Eric confessed. "Never know when they might be useful."

The twisted smile she gave him was genuine. "See, Coni." Hawke turned to look at the Kat's reflection. "I'm not the only one here with a fuckin brain."

"Because, of course, having grenades is the perfect way to sneak into a ship, steal its cargo and get away without being chased by the Sentries... Most likely Fleet Fighters." Coni's sarcastic tone drew a chuckle from Hawke.

Denthar, <Nope. Coni... You always need a grenade or two... it's—>

"Captains." Chris cut across the talking. "Space decompression." He leaned over his chair to reach the dataentry keys and tapped a few buttons on his console, highlighting another area of space on the windowscreen.

The convoy appeared in front of them. The effect of the vast ships slowing their engines from overdrive to standard propulsion made it look like they had warped into existence.

Eric gasped.

The windowscreen burst into a flurry of activity. Datawindows opened and shut, overlaying the ships and each other as the mainframe ran data too fast for Eric to read. Within seconds, one of the smaller transports highlighted and the windows closed, leaving the view of the stars and the convoy clear again.

Denthar, <Got the target and the bay.>

Hawke pushed at the controls, turning Werewolf towards the cargoship.

Denthar, <Ana?>

Ana, <Found an airlock, Captain.>

"Just keep up this time, Dent." Hawke's tone was scathing.

The convoy ship grew in the windscreen until its grey hull took up the entire view. Werewolf dodged sensors as she approached a set of cargobay doors. As she landed on the larger cargoship, there was pinging and clanking through the hull.

"Captain?" Coni's ears tracked the sound across the nearby wall.

Eric recognised the pings of gears contracting. They were hearing the echo of Werewolf as it settled on the hull of the other ship.

"Yeah, Con." Hawke stood and tested the draw of one of her guns. "We need to fix that. That noise will fuckin alert someone one standard." She thumbed at the pilot seat. "Don't let the kid screw with the settings."

Coni purred as she climbed over her console and jumped into Hawke's chair.

Hawke looked at Angel. "Don't move, kid."

Eric noted the look of pure innocence on the boy's face.

"I fuckin mean it."

Hawke started for the exit, motioning for Chris and Eric to join her.

As he followed, Eric glanced back. The boy had turned to Coni, giving her that same innocent expression. Eric shook his head and headed after the others.

They walked through the large space that was Werewolf's generator and equipment room towards the stairwell. As they headed down to the commonroom, Hawke tested the draw of her second gun, followed by her reach to a long, curved, tri-bladed serrated dagger, its sheath hooked into some loops on the back of her belt.

Eric grimaced at the cold metal, remembering the image of Xion.

"We move the crates whilst the captains take care of the bridge crew." Chris explained as they made their way into the centre cargobay.

Hawke swung around onto the ladder, gave Eric that dark smile and slid down on the outer rungs.

Chris motioned for him to follow. "There are more crates than we can fit, so we go for the target first, then any promising extras we find."

Eric and Chris climbed down after her.

"Why did the convoy leave FTL?" Eric joined Hawke at the large double doors on the floor of the space, while Chris went to their control console. "I mean, it would be safer to just stay in it."

Coni said, <They have returned to their route.>

Chris opened Werewolf's doors, then climbed down to look at the other ship's external controls for their bay. His tail stood straight up behind him as he concentrated on them.

"It is The Rim." Chris forced open the panel and pulled a few wires. "This entire sector of space is full of gravity wells, blackholes, starstorms... Makes navigating it completely—whilst in overdrive—a mess."

"Ok... So, why not just take the entire ship, kill the crew and sell the lot?" Eric leaned forward to watch the doors open with a slight whoosh of air. There was a burst from several ducts as Werewolf equalised the pressure.

"Ever tried to escape someone by walking when they can run?" Chris countered.

Eric glanced at Hawke, thinking about Chris's question.

She appeared oblivious to them. Instead, she was watching the doors, her eyes never blinking.

"The convoy security ships?"

"Yeah," Chris confirmed. "Smaller ships do not get as affected by the gravitational forces. That is why most convoys have smaller guard or troop ships. If we took a whole cargoship, they could hunt us down." His head poked up into the bay. "The bypass worked, Captains. The first they know of us should be your guns in their faces."

Denthar, <Ok. Let's move it. Ana, you have a map yet?>

Ana, <Yes, Captain. Chris, we are coming to you.>

Coni, <I have issued the passes. It is safe to enter Wolf.>

Eric turned slightly to look at Hawke again. She had that dark smile on her lips and had not moved as the crews worked. She inclined her head when she noticed his gaze.

Above them, the crane powered up. Small running lights blinked along its arm as it lowered towards the doors.

Chris tapped Eric's shoulder and pointed at the crane. "Our ride." Chris moved to a position to reach it easily.

Eric joined him, hooking the rifle over his head to allow the use of both hands.

Chris climbed onto the crane. Eric followed, turning to see what Hawke was doing.

She crouched at the edge of the doors, checked her angle and jumped into the other bay.

As the crane passed through the doorway, the gravity shift of 90 degrees gave Eric's stomach the flip-flops.

Hawke somersaulted across the grillwork and jumped over a stack of crates before sliding to a stop at the personnel entrance. The battery indicator on her gun lit up as she raised it in her hand and slipped through the door.

Chris directed Eric to follow him, and he dropped to the floor of the bay. The crane slowed and stopped. Eric stepped off and followed the Kat to the nearest stack of crates.

Denthar, <You takin a nap, Nina?>

"Already gone." Chris crouched, looking at the barcode on the nearest crate.

Denthar cursed.

Eric lifted the lid of a crate, checking its contents. He leaned over and picked up a part sitting on top. The diamond tipped drill bit was a familiar weight in his hand. It was sealed for protection in transportation, but the low lights still twinkled off the clear stone. Under it, the clamp that held the gem in place was resting. His eyes narrowed as he recognised the tan and blue stripe across it.

"Conda4s?" He looked at Chris, who nodded before they resealed the crate.

"Look for the crates with this sequence on them." Chris pointed at the middle six digits on the crate's barcode. "We get them all into Wolf as fast as we can."

Leaving questions until later, Eric helped Chris check the first few stacks of crates. It did not take long for them to figure out the order of the stacks and which ones they needed.

Denthar, <Stars, Nina, think you can hold off on the blood next time?>

Eric and Chris turned as they heard the personnel door slide open. Eric slipped the rifle around. He had it settled and aimed before Chris could shake his head at him.

"New one is jumpy." Shadows formed into a group of Terrans.

Eric recognised the voice as Ana. Her dark skin almost totally camouflaging her until she was right up next to them.

He lowered his rifle.

Denthar, <Two sequences with Hawke, you blame him?>

She looked up at Eric for a moment, then turned to the crates.

"Thought you were going silent, Captain?" She motioned to the rest of her crew to move the crates to the crane for transfer into Werewolf.

Chris smiled, metal teeth showing, and motioned for Eric to help with a crate.

Denthar, <No point. Nina's been practisin her knife work.>

Hawke said, <Bridge secure. Quit the fuckin chatter.>

Eric and Chris put a crate down while one of the other crewmembers wrapped the crane's lifting chains around the handles.

Ana chuckled and looked at Chris. "Your Captain."

Chris shrugged in return and turned to the piles of crates. "And she does not enjoy waiting."

Eric followed, heading for the next lot.

#

As he moved to get the next crate, Eric looked around the cargobay. The group had worked fast, shifting the crates they needed and a few extra they thought were promising. Two of Denthar's crew moved a larger crate towards the crane, growling and cursing at its weight.

Eric noticed a large stack of boxes in the corner, covered completely in shrink wrap to stop the smaller ones being separated. His interest soared when he realised they were the only set of items to have had that treatment. He walked over and crouched beside them.

The boxes were a dark grey that almost hid them in the shadows. Their sides were embossed with the flying eagle of UTC's fleet, their motto on a banner in its claws: *With Unity, Strength and Honour.*

"Found something?" Chris asked, joining Eric.

"No barcodes." Eric pulled at the shrink wrap. Tearing enough of it to get the first box out. He turned it around a few times, confirming none was there. "Might be worth a look."

Chris motioned to the others. "Ana, these as well."

Eric put the box back and helped them shift the entire package as one.

As it disappeared into Werewolf, Eric turned to Chris. "You know, every time there was unlisted Fleet gear on transports on Mars, there was Fleet."

Denthar said, <What was that? Nina! PAs—?>

His scream of pain left Eric's ear ringing.

They heard a curse from Hawke that the commlink did not translate and more than one energy blast crackled the speakers.

Chris bolted towards the personnel door, landing on all fours as he sped towards it.

Eric unslung his rifle and followed. The rush of adrenaline warmed his limbs. Glancing back at the door, he saw Ana not far behind.

"Bates, Zandi, Lander, get to the ship," Ana called back over her shoulder. "Pally."

Pally, <Coming.>

As they headed to the living areas of the ship Eric heard the energy blasts. He followed Chris, adjusting the rifle in his grip so it was ready to fire.

The Kat bounded through the airlock and leaped sideways to his right.

Eric skidded to a halt in the entrance to the large commonroom.

A power armoured suit lay face down on the floor. Electrical sparks and smoke poured out of its back, the burned smell of Terran flesh from its pilot spreading with it. Scattered around the space were tables and chairs, most melted, broken or glowing with heat.

Close to the entrance, Denthar was trying to stand. His arm was bent the wrong way and he coughed and wheezed in the commlinks.

A second PA suit stood near the middle of the room. The body it held had a ponytail of golden hair. The PA's gears whirred as it set its feet and threw Hawke across the room.

Eric watched her crash into the wall left of the door. The force dented the metal panel.

"Aim for the face shield," Eric told the others. "It scrambles their sensors." He followed Chris's path, clearing the doorway, firing a few shots at the suit.

Chris joined him, his rifle set, and fired some shots.

"Captain." Ana reached Denthar's side.

"Wait, my gun." Denthar struggled in Ana's grip.

"Leave it, Captain. I will buy you a new one."

"No." Denthar fought Ana's attempt to move him as he looked at Hawke. "Nina, move, for Sol's sake."

Eric heard a low groan that turned into a growl.

"Fuckin." Hawke pulled herself out of the dint in the wall and raised her dagger. "Chris, Hillar, distract it."

Eric kept his focus on the suit, while Hawke defied what he knew of force and bodily damage as she ran towards the PA.

Denthar and Ana stumbled towards the exit. Their crewmate had set up a defence at the open airlock, motioning for his captain and Ana to hurry.

The PA's cannon fired towards Chris.

He dropped on all fours to avoid impact. His rifle clattered from his grip. The Kat rolled before drawing his handgun. He fired a few shots, then got to a crouch. "Duck." He called out, drawing a second handgun from his thigh.

Eric dove to the grillwork, the PA firing at him. The energy blast warmed the back of his head and neck. He scrambled back to his feet. A few shots took the suit's attention from him and towards the door.

Hawke jumped, angling herself against the wall and then kicked off, landing on the suit's back.

Eric shot its faceplate again as she cut its powercabling.

With a dark grin, she dropped a burst grenade into the suit's cavity. "Fire in the hole."

A shiver ran down Eric's spine, hearing the pure malice in Hawke's words.

She climbed over the suit and leaped away. Hawke cursed in that untranslated language as the PA caught her ankle. It threw her towards the door.

Denthar pushed Ana away as Hawke crashed into him. They both tumbled through the open doorway as the others dropped to the floor, the explosion burning the surrounding air.

"That will just be the start." Chris warned, looking over at Eric. "There will be more guards coming."

Eric nodded and they turned towards the others.

Denthar laughed, the sound pained as Eric and Chris reached them in the corridor. He was sprawled across the grillwork, while Hawke slowly got to her knees beside him.

"You broke some ribs." Denthar groaned, accepting Ana's help off the ground.

Hawke slipped her dagger into its sheath. She shook her head, looking a little dazed.

"What's a few fuckin ribs?" She ignored Chris's offered hand and stood. "You're breathin. For now."

Coni, <They are preparing to drop out of FTL—I think they have called for help.>

"Never a dull rotation." Denthar saluted Hawke with a couple of fingers and let his crew help him towards their ship.

"Captain?" Eric slung his rifle as they headed for Werewolf.

"Still breathin." She sped up, gaining momentum. By the time they reached the cargobay, Hawke was far ahead of them.

She jumped through the airlock again and disappeared.

Eric followed Chris's lead and climbed onto the crane as the cargobay shook.

Hawke said, <Con?>

The crane lifted them into Werewolf. The cargobay doors slammed shut behind them.

Following Chris, Eric jumped to the grillwork, the crane continuing up into the shadows of the ceiling. The pair got to the ladder as a barrage of blasts shook Werewolf.

Coni, <Breaking electronic locks and getting out of your way.>

There was a humph from Hawke. <Get outta here, Dent.>

Chris clambered up the ladder, signalling Eric to follow.

Denthar, <Gotta protect my investment.>

Werewolf shook again.

Eric wrapped his arms around the rung, waiting for it to cease.

"Chris?" He looked up as the Kat tapped his commlink off.

Chris's grip was steady on the shaking rail.

"Breaking the electronic airlock between ships fries our shield for a minute. I need to get to the bridge to help get them back online." He tapped it back on before climbing again.

Denthar, <What in the stars?>

Hawke, <A whole fuckin wing.>

They reached the stairs to the bridge level. Chris bounded up them on all fours as Eric used the rail to speed his path.

Hawke, <We got some fucker's attention, Dent.>

Denthar, <Got a fix yet?>

Bates, <Something is scrambling our navicom.>

Eric reached the bridge as Chris plugged cables into his neck jacks.

The windowscreen turned as Hawke directed Werewolf in some crazy whirlwind path.

Coni was tapping at her console.

Werewolf shuddered from a direct hit. Eric staggered, catching himself on the backrest of the weapon's chair.

Angel watched from the copilot seat, his eyes on Hawke.

"That'll be the UTC Pursuer." Hawke pushed on her controls, sending Werewolf on a downward spiral. "Find her."

"If they are out there, they are good at hiding, Captain." Coni glanced back at Eric. He sat in the seat and looked at the controls.

Denthar, <You know we can see you?>

Hawke growled and whacked the console in front of her.

"Wolf."

Circuits rebooted from her impact. The navicom beeped but the indicators remained frozen.

"Shields back up." Chris's voice preceded the uptake from the generator in the room behind them. "Working on cloak."

The console near Eric was tracking fire and the ships in their proximity.

Hawke spat another curse as Werewolf turned again.

"There she is." Hawke's target appeared on the windowscreen and the datascreen above the weapon controls.

Denthar, <You can't take a Pursuit Class on. You don't even have a gunner.>

Eric looked up at Hawke's reflection. She was concentrating on the rapidly approaching Fleet ship. He looked back at the console and inhaled. A low burning anger built as he remembered another fight and the screams of those he could not save.

His hands moved to the triggers, the control of Werewolf's weapons transferred to him from the main console. He lined up the nearest fighter and fired. He was more than a little surprised when it hit.

The shot bounced off their shields but made the fighter jolt from the impact, throwing off their own targeting. On the screen, Eric saw Denthar's ship fly between them and the rest of the fighters.

"Your choice, Mr Hillar."

Eric smiled, hearing the dark enjoyment in her tone. He shot at another fighter.

Denthar, <Nina?>

"My turn." Hawke's growl reverberated across the bridge. The Fleet ship grew in the windowscreen.

"Captain!" Coni sunk into her chair as Hawke set them head on.

At the last second, the Pursuit ship turned, avoiding the collision by metres. On the console, a single target on the hull highlighted.

Eric fired before thinking.

"Get the fuck outta here, Dent." Hawke ordered.

The navicom whirred and its lights blinked from yellow to green. Computations ran across its datascreen.

Denthar, <Already gone.>

Eric saw the marker for Denthar's ship disappear off his datascreen. He looked up as the windowscreen burst into starlines. For a long moment, there was nothing but the sound of machines whirring on the bridge.

Hawke pulled her hands off the pilot controls and placed them on her armrests. She stared at the starlines.

Coni sat back in her chair, sighing loudly.

Chris sat up, unplugging the cables from the back of his neck.

"Fuck me," Hawke muttered, stretching her neck to the side.

Coni's posture went rigid and her ears pressed against her skull.

"Captain?" Coni climbed over her console to look over Hawke's shoulder.

"Nothing a glass of whiskey won't fix," Hawke groaned, stretching her back against the seat. "Or five."

"That is not exactly best medical practice."

Hawke laughed quietly, waving Coni's concern away and looked at Eric in the windowscreen's reflection. "Smart call on the grenades, Mr Hillar."

"You had them already."

She inclined her head and turned to the boy. "Kid?"

"I'm hungry." The innocent tone induced a laugh from the rest. "Burger?"

"Later."

Hawke stood, wavering for a moment before heading to the back of the bridge. She stopped to look at Eric when she reached the weapons console.

"Just what the fuck did you find?"

#

"Definitely a crystal generator, Captain." Chris looked up from the long clear column he had unwrapped from the Fleet packaging. "We will have to check if it is all here, but…" He trailed off as Hawke crouched next to the column and put her hand on it.

Eric saw her eyes reflected on the surface.

"Get it upstairs and check it." Hawke stood.

"Captain?" Chris blinked, looking at her. "What about…?"

"I'll deal with Dent." Hawke snorted, amused at some thought. "Who knows, we might have to call us even." She shrugged and looked up at the piles of crates in the surrounding bay. "You're up, Mr Hillar."

Eric took in the stacks. "That is a lot of crates," he mused. "Is it all Conda4 parts?"

"That's why you're fuckin here," Hawke growled. Her expression was not angry when he looked at her. "Check, sort, stack. You've got three sequences."

She patted Eric's shoulder as she walked passed him, heading for the ladder. "Good call on the suits."

Eric snorted. "You are the one who took one on with a dagger and a grenade."

She grunted, stepping onto the ladder.

Coni watched her, ears forward. "Captain?"

"Leave it." Hawke's tone of command was clear. She did not look back before she disappeared through the airlock to the living quarters.

Eric waited for Coni to turn back to them.

"How bad is she, Con?" Chris checked the crane straps around the generator boxes before heading to the console. He tapped a few commands, then watched the crane lift the whole package up to the ceiling.

"Hurt." Coni sighed and sat on the grillwork. "After what you said happened, she is lucky nothing got broken."

Eric blinked as doors in the ceiling retracted, the crane and cargo disappearing through it. As his gaze lowered back to the crates, he squared his shoulders.

"Well… No time like the present." He headed for a box.

"What's that?" Angel appeared beside him, pointing at the parts as Eric opened the first crate.

Eric blinked, lifting his arm to look at the boy next to him. He had not even noticed Angel had followed them.

Coni purred, waving at Angel to join her on the floor. "Angel…"

"It is ok." Eric showed the first part to the boy, letting him hold it and turn the metal around in his hands. "That is a coolant pump."

0.12

"Normally it would be me doin… How does Con put it? 'Holin up in the bridge and starin at the fuckin stars'." Hawke stopped between the chairs and looked down at Eric in the copilot seat.

He turned from the windowscreen and smiled at her. "You sure she would say 'fuck'?"

Hawke chuckled, passing him a tumbler of whiskey. She sat in her pilot chair and lifted her glass to have a drink.

Eric raised his own, wincing at the sizeable portion she had poured. "You could at least put ice in it."

"Ruins it."

Eric turned back to the starlines. He watched the ship draw close to a sun. Its line of light expanded in the windowscreen, then curved as Werewolf navigated around it, before disappearing. Several thinner lines appeared as the bright light faded from his eyes.

"I will never get used to this view." Eric leaned back in his chair, tumbler still in hand.

Hawke looked at the windowscreen before turning to her console.

"My girls would have loved to see this."

"Martian skies are too full of smog to see anything." Hawke put her glass on the navicom and began working something on the datakeys. "Not the best fuckin place to raise a kid."

"And a pirate ship is better?" Eric turned to look at her again, hearing her quiet laughter.

She turned her chair to look at him. "The kid is useful."

Eric gave into the urge to turn back to the windowscreen. Without thinking, he raised the drink and took a sip. The liquid scorched his throat. Coughing, he snorted the burn out of his nose.

"Was not expecting that," he confessed, looking at the glass again.

Hawke chuckled and took a big swig from her own. She looked down at the liquid left in her tumbler and shrugged.

"I must admit, life on a pirate ship is not what I expected either." Eric smiled as her eyebrows raised. "There is work, but it is not a constant grind. Not like the kitchen."

"The Tide always surprises." She hooked her boot up against the console and rested her elbow on her knee, watching the starlines turn. "Bit like on-the-run Martians that are tryin to hide their fuckin arses in plain sight as a cook."

"You will not let that go in a hurry, will you?"

"Nope."

Eric saw the smile before she hid it behind another drink.

"You are not exactly what the stories make out, either." He paused. When her only answer was another raised eyebrow, he went on. "Not exactly the cold killer everyone fears."

Hawke inclined her head, giving him that same icy gaze she had in Rebeal.

"People rarely fuckin are." She turned the tumbler in her hand, refracting the light from the starlines in the whiskey. "Judge on actions, not reputation. Speakin of, you've earned a bonus for findin that generator... and the backup with the PAs and Pursuer."

Eric's brow furrowed slightly.

"I didn't bring you in for combat. I didn't expect you to," Hawke finished.

"Yeah, well. I never enjoyed sitting on the sidelines. Probably why I got caught up in the troubles on Mars." He watched her carefully, trying to gauge her reaction to his next question. "Enough to disappear?"

Her snort was answer enough.

"Did not think so." Eric looked at the quiet bridge, then at the copilot controls in front of him. "What happens back at Sirius?"

"You still thinkin of tryin to hide your fuckin arse as a cook?" Her contempt turned the word into a curse.

Eric inhaled, staring at the windowscreen.

"No."

Something eased in his mind and chest when he voiced it. The pressure he had put on himself to change seemed to be lessoning.

"Honestly, I just ran. Did not really think about what to do once I got out of UTC space. Just let things fall into place around me on Sirius. Not to mention being recruited for this."

"Used to havin your whole fuckin existence dictated to you." She ran her hand over her ponytail as she stared out the window. "Known a few like you. Too used to the UTC in command, being told what to do, when to piss, or if they can even fuckin stick it somewhere."

"No argument there." Eric tried a smaller sip. Now he was expecting it, the whiskey did not burn so much. "In a way, they dictated the uprising. Running was just about the only thing I did that was not forced on me."

He heard another snort.

Hawke leaned to the side of her seat and pulled up a bottle from somewhere in the console. She refilled her drink.

"If you call that fuckin farce, runnin."

"And you know better, Captain?" Eric tugged at his goatee. "I expect you would not even know the concept of running." He paused when he saw the familiar dark smile appear.

"If you're really runnin... I mean, down to your fuckin bones runnin, Mr Hillar, you would've made for Tombstone, not Sirius. Sirius gets people's attention. Gets you on the sensors of fuckers like me. Gets you in a spot where you can make more noise and send those fucks in the UTC your very own brand of fuck you."

"Tombstone?" Eric blinked, surprised. "It does not exist."

"It does." Hawke swirled her drink. "But that's not where you want to be. You aren't cut out for that life."

"What kind of life? Hard work and simple needs?"

"A cage."

"Cage?"

"Tombstone is a cage." She drank before continuing. "Yes, it's powerful enough to be neutral even out here on The Rim. No one will dare threaten her or those on her. But once you're there, what then?"

"Some people choose a quiet—"

She cut him off with a dismissive wave of her hand, adjusted her angle, stretched and dumped her feet on the navicom. "You won't be happy with that. Not until you figure out what the fuck you really are."

"And you know what you are?" Eric countered.

"A pirate."

He sat back, watching her as he processed the answer. "Pirate?"

She inclined her head at his tone, giving him that twisted smile again.

"I raid, I steal, and I kill any fucker that looks at me, my crew or my ship in a manner I don't fuckin like. I'm a pirate." The starlines reflected in her eyes as she looked at them. "Until you understand how far you're willin to go to stay free, you'll always be hidin from yourself."

Eric took another sip of whiskey, deciding, like Hawke, it was harsh but not entirely bad.

"Free from what?" He looked at the scar on his wrist, then back to Hawke.

"Name that fucker." Hawke shrugged. "If it's not bounty hunters or slavers, it's some fuckin authority or another. Let others decide your place in the stars or do it yourself."

"And you, Captain? What made you choose?"

"Maybe one rotation you'll find out." She drank again, emptying her glass. "And maybe fuckin not."

Eric stared at her for a minute before bursting into laughter. That belly-deep, relaxing laughter he had not felt in a long time.

"You find me amusin?" She looked surprised but responded with a chuckle. "I guess I fuckin am."

"Only a little, Captain." Eric wiped the tears from his face, regaining control, although he let his smile remain. "Just remembered what you said to Denthar in Rebeal, about history lessons."

"He needs to learn not everyone enjoys bein a fuckin open datascreen."

"Well… you helped me out." He shrugged. "Thanks."

She blinked at him.

"Not used to having someone grateful?"

"Not used to doin somethin someone would be fuckin grateful for."

"Well, I am." Eric looked at the starlines. "And I am certainly glad to have seen this."

"You are one fuckin piece of work, Mr Hillar."

"I have my moments, Captain." Eric looked up at Werewolf's ceiling. "And, as thanks, I might be able to help you out. Wolf's got what? A double hull?" He turned back to her, smiling as her eyes narrowed. "That is why you get those echoes from the landing gear?"

"Triple." Her tone was cautious.

"We had a way of packing the hulls in the diggers." He shrugged. "Was a field modification, not on the specs. It might help."

Hawke sat up in her chair, her chin angled, focusing on him. "With what?"

"We had rubber, but anything non-metal or wave absorbing should work."

She hmphed and turned back to the starlines. "Chris said you're done with the checks."

Eric leaned back in his chair and followed her gaze. The many colours of the starlines flooded over his face.

"Six complete Conda4s—minus the standard battery packs, of course." He rested the glass in his lap. "Plus a few handheld tools that come in handy under the rock."

"Batteries aren't our fuckin problem." She dismissed the missing component with a flick of her fingers. "We've got a sequence to the rendezvous. Consider it leisure time after you show me this packin technique."

Eric laughed and leaned forward to look at the copilot console. He raised his hands and paused, staring at the dataentry keys. She was staring at him again when he looked at her.

"How do you get the Conda4 specs up on this thing?"

Hawke chuckled as she tapped a few keys on her console.

A datascreen window opened in front of Eric. He pointed at the cross-section in the machine's hull.

#

Chris showed Eric the hidden compartment in his leg. The thigh parted in two as the skin weave separated to reveal the holster. Around it, the wires and gears of his leg moved as Chris adjusted his balance. With a smooth movement, he slipped the gun back into its holster and the two sections of skin folded back over. Once he smoothed the fur down, Eric could not see a break in it or the skin.

"And you also have the side holster and visible gun," Eric nodded appreciably. "Nice misdirect."

"Never been caught unarmed." Chris sat back at the table and picked up his fork. He twirled the spaghetti onto it and took a large bite. "It has come in handy," he mouthed around the food.

They heard Coni sigh from the couch. She was reading a datapad, her legs curled up under her. Beside her, Angel was finishing his own bowl of spaghetti.

Hawke was sitting opposite Chris and Eric, her attention on one of her guns. She had pulled the casing off and was checking the circuit inside with a fine-pointed screw. Beside her was a tumbler of whiskey and the untouched bowl Eric had placed next to her. The sound of her tool stopped as she looked up at the mainframe. She clicked the casing shut and stood. Powering up the gun, she headed for the stairs.

"Get ready for company." There was an edge to her tone. "Meetin Charger in a few."

"Does she have cybernetics or something?" Eric looked at the mainframe as a starchart appeared on one screen. "I mean, to connect to Werewolf?"

"Think so." Chris stood. "I will get the airlock. Con?"

"Captain will activate the passes once she is happy it is them." Coni did not look up from her datapad.

Eric watched Chris disappear down the personnel airlock. He turned to Coni.

"Airlock?"

"Wolf and Charger have universal airlocks. Means they can link in-flight to transfer crew or supplies."

"If she is reliant on another crew to do bigger jobs, why not just bring more people into Werewolf?"

Coni looked up at his question.

"It is not like you cannot fit them." Eric added.

She opened her mouth to answer but closed it as she looked behind him, her ears folding.

"Why not just hire more on, Dent?" Hawke had returned from the bridge. She leaned against the stair rail as Denthar appeared with Chris and three of his crew at the entrance.

"Because you're a paranoid bitch." Denthar chuckled and rubbed at his shoulder. A brace strapped his arm to his chest and there was no gunbelt on his waist.

Hawke crossed her arms. "Because, Mr Hillar, most arses on The Rim are power hungry fucks, and I don't share command." She shrugged while Denthar laughed.

Chris sat at the mainframe, while two of Denthar's crew placed a large bag on the floor before joining Eric near the table.

"Captain." The one Eric recognised as Bates, placed a bottle of whiskey on the table. "To compensate for the intrusion for the next few hours."

"You givin them tips, Dent?" Hawke raised her eyebrows at Denthar.

"Maybe."

"Arm?"

"Broken."

"Medivi?"

"Don't have any."

Hawke snorted. "You went into a fight with no fuckin Medivi on board?" She shook her head.

"It isn't as easy to get recently," Denthar confessed, rubbing the back of his neck. "A lot of the supplies seem to have dried up." Hawke's dark chuckle induced a sharp look from him. "You didn't?"

"Con."

"Give me a minute, Captain." Coni put her datapad down and bounded over the couch and down the stairs.

"Nina, seriously?" Denthar was staring at her. "Varsely's already pissed at you. You had to provoke him?"

"Varsely is a misogynist fuck." Hawke dismissed Denthar's concern. "Me breathin provokes him." She looked at Denthar's crew standing around the commonroom. "Sit the fuck down."

There was a general laugh as they found chairs around the end of the table.

Eric glanced around at them. They were all Terrans. One appeared to be a mixed subspecies. They were blue-skinned with the same tint to their hair and almond-shaped eyes. Another was a Canis. His ears pointed but not able to move like the Kats.

Bates sat down and pulled out a small device and a deck of cards. He looked at Eric.

"Game?" Bates setup the device as his crewmates moved into positions to see it.

"Depends. What are you thinking?" Eric moved his empty bowl aside, watching Bates shuffling.

Coni reappeared with one of her medical guns.

"Hold still, Captain."

Denthar braced himself as she injected his upper arm.

"Give it a few hours and you will be right."

Denthar nodded.

"Called Poker. You have probably never heard of it."

Bates had that self-assured air that sent Eric's skin tingling in warning.

In the corner of his vision, he saw Denthar look at Hawke, his expression sharp.

She smiled and she motioned something at the other captain. Hawke moved forward and grabbed her tumbler from the table, before resuming her spot at the stairs.

Eric saw the tiny incline of her head and it was all the encouragement he needed.

"Heard of it..." Eric tapped his chin. "I am more of a triple draw player myself."

Denthar had a sudden fit of coughing, while Hawke drank her whiskey.

"Something about playing for the largest count?" Eric tried for a look of thought. "Four of a kind and flushes or something?"

Bates nodded. "That is it." He started dealing the deck. "We will show our hands for a few rounds so you can get the hang of it."

Eric nodded, watching the cards slide across the table towards him.

They played a few rounds, with Bates explaining the cards and their combinations.

As Eric flipped over his last card, there was an appreciative noise from the others.

"Nice," said Bates. "Two aces and three nines. That is a full house; you win." He picked up the cards and shuffled them.

"How about we play for real now?" The Canis asked. He leaned over the table and offered his hand to Eric. "I'm Paladin, by the way."

Eric shook Paladin's hand, taking in his brown fur and the simple grey jumpsuit he wore.

"Need to say, never seen someone deliberately put themselves against a PA suit," Paladin added, his voice tinted with admiration.

"You missed the bit where this crazy decided it was a fun idea." Denthar pointed a thumb at Hawke.

"Next time, I'm fuckin runnin and leavin you for dead." She raised her eyebrow at him.

"Who are you kiddin?" Denthar bantered back. "You don't know how to run."

"We playing or not?" Bates asked, looking at Eric.

Eric noticed the others had slipped creditdisks into the device.

"I did not exactly collect my pay before leaving Rebeal." Eric shrugged.

"I'll spot him."

They turned to Hawke, surprised.

She gave them that twisted smile. "Chris."

"Guess the Captain has money to burn." Chris slid a disk into the device when he reached Eric's side.

Eric only just stopped himself from laughing as he saw the cyborg wink.

#

"Four of a kind, people." Bates laid his cards down on the table at the collective groans from the others. "Thank you for participating." He leaned forward to tap the device to collect.

"Hold it." Eric put his own cards down. "Straight flush."

"Wait… what?" Bates blinked and Denthar laughed, thumping him on the back.

There was a snort from Hawke.

Bates looked up at Denthar, rubbing his shoulder.

"Captain?"

"Three draw is Poker." Denthar was still laughing. "Martians have a lot of downtime in dark caverns."

"And you did not think to warn me?"

"What? And miss that expression on your face?" Denthar smiled at Eric. "Although I wasn't expectin Nina to step in."

They turned to her as she raised her glass and saluted Eric.

"Well, aren't we all full of fuckin surprises?" She turned to walk up the stairs. "Get ready. We're almost at the colony."

O.13

Eric pulled his jacket into place as he reached the top of the stairs to the commonroom.

Denthar and his crew had their bag on the table and were sorting out their guns.

Eric checked the draw of his handgun and settled the rifle against his shoulder.

"Nice jacket," Bates observed.

Eric looked up and smiled. "No. Not playing for it."

"He's got you fuckin figured already, Bates." Hawke glanced at something on the mainframe before going back to checking the draw of her guns.

"We must credit him with brains, Captain. He has survived you so far." Bates paused when Hawke looked at him, her face cold in its complete lack of expression.

"If I kill you all, who do I terrorise?" She motioned to Eric. "You're with Dent and me," she told him. "They may want info on those diggers."

"Who are 'they'?"

"Mining colony." Denthar wrapped the strap of a rifle around his good arm. "No affiliates, just people tryin to survive out here."

"I'd rather sell through Zeb, but Dent has a fuckin soft spot for hard cases," Hawke muttered. She drew her dagger and tested its edge.

"Good thing or you wouldn't have a crew," Denthar countered. "Honest, hard-workin folk, that's all, Hillar."

"You better be fuckin right about the deal." Hawke started for the personnel airlock. "Chris is in the cargobay." She thumbed at the other airlock, looking at Bates, Paladin and the others. "Con'll let you know when to offload."

Hawke waited until she was alone with Eric and Denthar in the corridor. "If we offload." She glared at Denthar and sighed.

Denthar rolled his eyes. "We'll get more here than with Zeb. You're always so paranoid about new people."

"For valid fuckin reasons."

"Just let me do the talkin. You stand back and glower... We might get more creds if you do."

Denthar moved ahead, not noticing the silent snort from Hawke.

Eric tried to wipe the smile from his face as they reached the airlock.

Hawke inclined her head, confirming Eric's suspicion that she had wanted Denthar to do the talking. Her ease of playing Denthar to get what she wanted struck Eric as cold, but also strangely companionable.

She tapped her commlink onto auto and motioned for Eric to do the same, leaving Denthar to open the airlock.

He turned his commlink on and walked down the ramp.

The personnel ramp lowered onto the grillwork of an enormous hangar. The area had only a few boxes and crates near some doors at the far end of the space. Werewolf had landed in the centre of the dock. Behind her engines, the blue light of the electronic airlock tinted the stars and sky beyond. The place was empty of people.

As Eric followed the captains to the bottom, he heard the whirling of gears. He looked back, watching two rifles unfold from Werewolf's hull, their indicators blinking to red as their sensors tracked him. The airlock shut and he heard the small beep in his commlink. The rifles moved to cover the surrounding hangar.

Eric had been on Werewolf for just over five sequences but had never seen her exterior. She was not a pretty ship. There were no streamlines or atmospheric curves to her. She was a cargoship, built for long hauls across the galaxy. From what he could see of the hull, it was pitted with damage from heat and impacts. The panelling was mismatched from recent and past replacements and riddled with compartments and sensors.

Moving further away from her, Eric caught sight of one engine. At three-stories high, it dominated his vision with the power glow of the exhaust. Werewolf was nothing like the slim, sleek looking Fleet Pursuit Class she had faced down or Denthar's ship, Charger.

"She's got a few surprises."

Hawke was watching him. He swallowed and lowered his gaze, checking the reach of his rifle, looking for time to make a response.

"Surprises?" Denthar snorted. "She would have to with the amount of money you've sunk into her."

"Where the fuck are they, Dent?" Hawke looked around the bay.

Eric followed her gaze.

"The colony entrance is that way." Denthar pointed at the far wall with the crates and the doors. "Maybe they've heard how Wolf doesn't like feelin crowded?" He headed towards the closed airlock doors. "You two are prone to shootin people. Maybe they just want to stay outta your range?"

Eric looked at Hawke. He heard the quiet tapping.

She watched Denthar, her hands resting on her guns. One finger tapped a plain ring against the handle. She noticed Eric watching and shrugged, pulling her hands from the guns but left them close.

As they approached, a short, thin creature with long, sinewy arms and a bright orange mane came through the doorway. They stopped and waited for the group to reach them.

"Sorry for the delay in meeting you," they spoke, waving their arms for them to follow out of the bay.

Hawke looked back at her ship once.

Eric saw her commlink blink a sequence before she nodded at him and moved to follow Denthar and the creature.

Chris said, <I am getting into the network now.>

Denthar looked at Hawke, eyes narrowing.

<It has a difficult firewall… Give me a minute.>

"We have recently transferred management here." The creature seemed oblivious to their actions. "It has been a bit of a logistical mess. No one seems to remember anything about doing their job."

"Maybe we should take our goods elsewhere?" Denthar said. "The new management might not want—"

"No, no. Was your message correct, Conda4s?"

Denthar nodded.

"We are still interested. I believe it was 100,000 trade credit each?"

Eric noticed movement in the shadows of an offshoot corridor. His guts twisted and his fingers tightened on his rifle's grip. The quiet of the mining colony was wrong. Where were the workers? Their families? Even the lights were low when they should be at to their brightest, allowing for sight in the heavy mining suits needed for dangerous materials.

Beside him, Hawke's shoulders tensed, her eyes narrowed. She closely watched the alien ahead of them. Her low growl only formed into a word in Eric's commlink.

"Coni?"

Bates said, <She is concentrating on something, Captain... She mentioned a subchannel.>

Eric angled his rifle. He flicked the safety off. The battery indicator lit up the side of the barrel.

Hawke nodded at Eric, her hands back on her guns.

Paladin, <We have signalled Charger.>

"In here, please." The creature led them into a large conference room. The table along one side was ivory white with a slight glow. "I will get the master." They slipped out of a door on the other side of the room.

"Master?" Denthar breathed. "Nina..."

Eric stiffened as he heard the lock click.

Denthar spun, lifting his rifle. He lowered it when he saw they remained alone.

Hawke was glaring at the doorway the alien disappeared through.

"I smell—." She screamed.

The pitch coming through the commlinks was high enough to make Eric and Denthar stagger.

Hawke dropped to her knees, her hand clutching the side of her head.

Eric winced. His commlink shot a series of random noises through his head, then crackled to silence. He looked at Denthar, recognising the static of a comms blackout.

Denthar's rifle dangled from his good arm and he caught himself against the table.

"Nina?" Denthar turned from her as they heard the doors open.

Eric spun around, rifle raised. He backed up slowly as a row of men filed in, arranging themselves along the walls of the room, rifles loaded and aimed. They wore brown uniforms that Eric recognised from revolutions of news propaganda. The crosscut jackets were lightly armoured and they held their rifles in the same ready position. Their slightly green skin and different degrees of red to brown hair identified them as Alati.

"Give her a minute there, Captain Denthar."

"Varsely?" Denthar looked around the room.

Eric swept his rifle across the line of soldiers, waiting for Varsely to present himself. As he breathed, he noticed a strange, slightly sweet smell fill the room.

"Someone had to take over management of this mineral-rich solar system."

Varsely appeared then, materialising from behind the row of soldiers.

The Alati stood in front of Hawke, looking down at her. Their violet-coloured eyes matched Varsely's suit. The smile on his face was cruel and his eyes flickered to the hand that was pressed against her head.

"I fear I may have scrambled her cybernetics a little with that signal." Varsely snorted as he continued to stare at Hawke. "She will need a minute to recover... If she ever does."

Hawke was breathing hard, staring at the grillwork in front of her. Her other hand held her steady as she leaned on her knees.

Denthar's eyes narrowed. The captain swallowed and straightened, regripping his rifle. His stance tensed, his muscles flexing as he adjusted his feet.

"So, this is the Martian." Varsely looked at Eric. "You owe me for the crew you killed on Sirius and for helping Hawke find my supply lines. A few years in a slave collar should repay that debt."

"We came to deal." Denthar inhaled and continued. "If you don't want to buy, fine. We'll—."

"I am buying." Varsely cut him off with a dismissive wave. "Or rather I am taking, Captain. I think this woman owes me a few things. She knows better than to steal from me. I want compensation."

Denthar's eyebrow raised.

"I think those diggers and that ship of hers will be payment for the Medivi she stole. Hawke, you have a choice to make: Marhend, Alatis or UTC. I'll let you have your pick... Even though Alati command is paying more."

"Vars—"

"Things are changing out here, Captain." Varsely continued, ignoring the warning in Denthar's tone. He took a step forward. "You will be smart to—"

A growl of pure anger, promising violence, crackled through the room.

"Get down!" Hawke bellowed, knocking Varsely's feet from under him. He crashed to the grillwork.

Denthar and Eric dropped to the floor, the room lighting up with energy bullets.

Hawke's dagger slid into Varsely's spine in one smooth movement. Drawing a gun, she fired down the blade's length, the energy dissipating into Varsely's skin. She grabbed fistfuls of his hair as she tore the blade free. Lifting the back of his head, she slammed his face into the grillwork.

Hawke rolled over him, heading towards the table. Both guns came up first, already firing, as she crouched. Her jacket took a few direct hits. The Alatis' screams filled the room, along with the acrid smell of cooked meat and the tinge of her smouldering jacket.

Eric dodged and returned fire, falling back to scramble under the table.

Denthar was already there. He dropped the rifle, fitting his handgun in his good hand.

Eric pulled his own handgun out and fired at the legs he could see.

It was messy, loud and fast. Within seconds, Eric was lowering his gun and moving back out into the open.

Hawke had not even bothered to dodge. Her jacket was smoking in places, but she appeared physically unharmed.

"Captain?" Eric stood and he reached her side before offering a hand up.

She ignored it. Instead, she growled, struggling to stand as she forced her legs to function.

Eric glanced around the room, seeing the dead Alati soldiers, the destroyed chairs and the blackened scars on the top of the table.

"Fuckin… fuck. Fuck." Hawke shook her head and leaned against the table. "You fuck, Varsely."

"Well, you always could illustrate the diversity of that word." Denthar rolled his eyes and snorted.

"Fuck you, Dent."

Eric laughed silently. He then helped Denthar to stand and handed him his dropped rifle.

Near them, Varsely groaned.

"He's alive?" Denthar blinked, staring at Varsely's prone form. "Why?"

"We need info." Hawke stared through the open door from her spot against the table. "Dent, get a jack into that console." She pointed towards the other room.

Eric looked at what she was pointing at. Through the doorway, there was a large command console with a wall of datascreens and an internal airlock that led to another section of the colony.

Denthar took a small, finger-length computer jack Hawke held up as he passed her.

Hawke pulled the commlink out of her ear, looked at the dead indicator light, then tossed it away. Eric smiled as she pulled a new one out of a belt container and fitted it in. The commlink lit up as it booted.

"What was that in the comms?" Eric asked, nudging Varsely's shoulder with his boot. The man groaned. He looked at Hawke as she turned back to the Alati on the floor.

"High frequency jammer." Hawke's tone was firming. "Didn't expect something that high-tech from this fuck." She rubbed a gun barrel against her temple. "Wolf'll be back soon. They need to reboot the system. You two were fuckin lucky. Those idiots were only thinkin about my bounty."

"Well, it's temptin. You gotta give them that." Denthar laughed from the other room.

"Bit of a knock?" Eric indicated her temple when she looked at him.

"Scrambled the fuckin brains, that's for sure." Her gaze followed Denthar as he moved from the console and headed to the airlock.

The jack blinked in its slot.

"Dent, did that fuck say Marhend?"

"Yeah. Why?" Denthar tried to move the handle. "It's locked. Got a pick or something? There's a reed point here." Denthar ran his finger over the frame. "Yep, can definitely get this open—"

Denthar jumped at the sound of a single shot. The control panel next to him melted from the blast. The airlock hissed slightly, and the seals deflated. He shot a dark look towards her. "Nina," he protested.

"Looks like this freehold isn't a freehold anymore." She slid her gun back into its holster.

"Those were soldiers." Eric glanced around the room.

"Yeah." She blinked as they heard another few beeps from the commlinks.

Coni, <Back online... And, Captain, we have a problem. Wolf's...>

Hawke looked at the ceiling before tapping her link on.

"Chris, reset stacks four, 19 and 27. That'll bring her back online." She looked at the computer jack in the console as it blinked several times. "And be ready to open stacks 32 to 35."

Coni, <And, that subchannel...>

Hawke looked down.

Eric followed her gaze. They watched Varsely's form as his hand twitched.

"Is it an Alati Patrol Class or Corvette?"

Coni, <Corvette.>

Hawke nodded as Denthar looked along the corridor.

"We're safe here but the minute we move, they'll be on us." Denthar looked back at them. "Check your weapons."

Eric turned his rifle to look at the battery indicator: *80%*.

Hawke's eyes remained on the Alati. "Dent?"

"Hmm?"

"Did you ever mention Wolf or me when settin the deal up?"

"No… Why?"

"Cause I'm thinkin, that fuckin arse was goin to deal with you." She staggered a little before she crouched next to Varsely. She rolled him over and started checking his pockets. "And this was just a fuckin opportunity."

"We need to move." Denthar looked back down the corridor. "Just kill him already."

Eric joined Hawke next to Varsely. She pulled a creditdisk out from his inner jacket pocket. She showed it to Eric, the lights catching the fine lines and triangles of the embossing. Eric inclined his head, remembering another ambush and another disk.

"Better the fuck you know, Dent." She tapped Varsely's cheek with the card before slipping it into her own pocket. "Thought you fuckin knew that."

Hawke stood and motioned for Eric to follow as she walked, a little unsteadily, out of the room to the console.

"Back at Sirius, Coni found something on that slaver when I…" Eric trailed off, following her.

Hawke inclined her head at him and leaned against the console.

"Datadisk with that fuck's trade routes." Her grin was full of sharp teeth. "Why would I kill him when I can profit off him?" She turned to the jack. Its light changed from green to orange. "Chris?"

Chris, <Uploading colony's data now, Captain.>

"And the soldiers?" Denthar sounded sceptical.

"He mentioned minerals." Eric shrugged at the other captain. "Palladium? There is a lot of money in that. Alatis might be trying to set up their own supply chain."

Chris, <That would explain the sudden technology upgrade too, if Varsely is dealing with military. Upload done. I'll have the map in a few.>

"No rush." Hawke checked her guns. "We're already surrounded. It's just a matter of deciding which fucks we go through."

"If I had armour like that, I guess I would not worry either." Eric motioned at her jacket.

She glanced at a new soot mark on her forearm.

"We can't all lead charmed fuckin lives," she countered.

Eric glanced at himself, realising what she was looking at: his clean unmarked jacket.

"I think they were all aiming for you this time, Captain."

Her snort confirmed his suspicions.

"How many do you think?" Eric asked.

"Corvette is a personnel carrier." She put her hand on the jack in the console. "Max, 12 troops of six."

"We took out 12 in there," Denthar added. "So, you're sayin possibly 60 more?"

Eric was certain he saw that glimmer across Hawke's eyes.

"Nina?"

"Hmm?"

"Would Wolf let Bates fly her?"

Hawke fixed Denthar with a blank look.

He shrugged and pointed at the corridor. "We could swing round to a different bay if they can move her."

"I am surprised they have not gone after the ship already," Eric added quietly, moving over to Denthar near the corridor.

Eric leaned against the wall, settling his rifle against his side. He looked up at the laughter from the crews through his commlink.

Hawke gave him that twisted but genuine smile again.

The jack light turned green. Hawke pulled it out and slipped it back into her belt container. "Bates?"

Bates said, <Werewolf, like her captain, does not like to have someone getting too friendly with her. What is the exclusion, Captain? 100 metres?>

"If we're in a good mood." Hawke joined them at the door. She pressed her fingers to a temple and closed her eyes. The light in her commlink flickered green, red, white, then back to green. "Don't you dare fuckin dint her."

Bates, <I would never... But the Alatis might be stupid enough to get in the way. I cannot promise about them.>

Denthar snorted and shrugged.

Hawke rolled her eyes.

Bates, <Zander, get on the copilot. Paladin—>

Paladin, <Guns.> His voice raised in excitement. <Always wanted to check this targeting system out.>

"Don't get fuckin used to it." Hawke looked at Eric. "Raid, steal, kill."

"Funny." Eric set his rifle on his shoulder.

"Do you hear me laughin?" Her amused tone almost did exactly that.

Eric smiled, not bothering to answer.

Coni, <We are out of the dock and circling.>

Denthar nodded, readying his rifle.

Hawke looked at the pair of them. "Alatis are gun fodder," she muttered and pulled her guns out. "They don't train them to aim, just to pull the trigger, but that won't fuckin matter in the corridor. Move fast and hold your fire until the last moment."

"Where are we going?" Eric asked.

Chris, <500 metres to your left is a stairwell. Three flights up and across to another dome is an airlock we can attach to.>

Hawke looked down the sight of her gun.

"Nina?"

"I'm good. That fuckin signal rattled the brains." She raised her guns to shoulder height and gave Denthar a cold smile. "First Fleet, then Alatis… You're spoilin me on this one."

She spun out into the corridor, guns aimed.

"Don't mention it." Denthar rolled his eyes, sarcasm dripping from his words. He and Eric followed, their rifles interchanging between behind and in front as they swapped directions on the slow walk.

The quiet was strange to Eric. A mining colony should be full of noise. People moving from area to area, machines going, goods being moved from manufacturing to storage or other spaces. "Where is everyone?"

Chris, <Down in the refinery areas, under guard by the looks.>

"Not our fuckin problem." Hawke spoke through her teeth.

Coni, <They are closing in. Move.>

They broke into a run, turning a corner and skidding to a halt at the doorway to the stairs.

"This feels wrong." Eric looked up the centre of the stairwell. He saw nothing, but his guts were telling him they were there. "Ambush?"

"Fuck it." Hawke ran the short landing to the stairs and jumped onto the first half flight. She rolled across the grillwork and pressed her back against the wall, her guns pointed up.

Denthar signalled to Eric and they joined her quickly.

Edging around the landing, Hawke put a foot on the next stair.

A fist-sized canister rattled down the stairs, bouncing on its ends as it fell towards them. The light it blinked was red as it clicked and dinged.

Eric jumped forward and grabbed it as the cylinder bounced high on their landing. Turning, he threw it down the corridor they came through.

Hawke pushed Denthar up the stairs with the butt of her gun pressed against his back. With her other one, she aimed at the canister.

"Hillar, run."

Eric scrambled after Denthar. Behind him, he heard Hawke's gun fire. The stairwell shook as the blast heated the surrounding space. The rush of smoky hot air pushed him off balance. He slipped, landing heavily on his knees.

Hawke reached Eric's side and hooked an arm under his shoulder. She lifted him and pushed him towards Denthar again, before turning back to face the stairwell.

Eric stumbled through the next doorway, along with Denthar, into a corridor. Coughing and fighting for fresh air, Eric heard Hawke's guns firing, the sound of men cursing and returning fire. The other side of the corridor's wall was viewing glass, showing the mining colony spread out below them, the stars in their inky-black sky above.

"Sol," Denthar cursed. He raised his rifle, aiming at the far end of the corridor and the intersection there. "Nina?" He grunted as her back pressed against theirs, jolting him and Eric with force.

Hawke's guns fell silent as she aimed at the doorway to the stairs.

Eric looked in the opposite direction and pointed his rifle.

A mass of brown uniforms and powered up rifles greeted him.

"Drop your weapons," one of the Alatis ordered.

Eric felt Hawke's back vibrate against him as she growled.

"No fuckin chance."

Eric looked towards the window again. The pale blue sun was rising over the moon's horizon. As he watched, the soft light reflected off several small fighters circling the colony. Their moves seemed deliberate, as if they were sweeping the area, looking for something.

"Hawke." He breathed the word. Her head turned slightly, just enough for him to see the edge of her face. He nudged his chin towards the window. "Would that collar work?"

The grin that spread across her face was dark and cold.

"I said, drop—"

"Shut the fuck up." She snarled back at the Alati.

Eric saw that sequence of green, red, and even white in her commlink again.

Chris, <Seriously?>

Bates, <I can do that. Pally?>

Paladin, <With Wolf's targeting… Yes.>

There was a shimmer against the black of space. The cloak from Werewolf's hull peeled away from her in a burst of colour. Behind her, Eric saw the Alati fighters scatter as Charger suddenly appeared inside their formation, guns firing.

Several Alati soldiers rattled orders, but when the first shot from Werewolf hit the corridor's window, their command disintegrated. Air hissed as Werewolf's rifles made quick work of the glass.

"Hold on and exhale." Hawke spun on a heel, holstering her guns. She grabbed Denthar and Eric each by their upper arm and kicked off the grillwork as the vacuum of space forced the air out of the corridor.

Eric saw the grey of Werewolf's panels and heard the sucking as his ears popped.

Eric had the terrifying vision of unprotected space. His muscles froze and his lungs burned from lack of air pressure. Hawke's grip on his arm was a vice. Heat tingled across his body from the contact, pins and needles bit into his skin.

Werewolf's personnel entrance appeared in front of them. The bright white of her lights tinged blue from the electronic airlock that kept her pressurised.

Energy covered Eric as they catapulted through the airlock.

Hawke's grip on his arm tightened, her feet landing on the inner wall, breaking their speed into the ship's corridor.

Eric's shoulder hit the metal panelling of the wall. Hawke's grip prevented his face from smashing into it. He stumbled a little, catching his balance. He registered Denthar looking at him, the gravity of Werewolf and then Hawke's grip lessening.

Instinctively, he grabbed for her forearm, Denthar doing the same. Hawke's weight drew a gasp from him, pulling them off balance, as her back crashed on to Werewolf's grillwork.

The airlock door shut.

It locked, and Eric felt the engines rotate up as Werewolf jumped into overdrive.

Bates, <We are gone!>

Denthar laughed, letting go of Hawke, and leaned against the wall.

Eric blinked, staring at her on the grillwork. He joined Denthar, sliding down the wall to a sitting position and reassessed her. She was tall and did not have a light frame, but certainly did not look as heavy as she was.

Hawke shook her head as she sat up, pulling her arms free to lean back on them.

"Sol, Nina. Varsely's gonna be pissed when he wakes up." Denthar breathed a sigh.

"Most fuckin likely." She pulled out the creditdisk and showed Denthar before slipping it away again. She then looked at Eric. "Good work, Hillar."

"You'd make a decent pirate if you wanted to. Good instincts and not afraid of the crazies," Denthar agreed. "There better be something decent on that."

"If not, I'll finish what I fuckin started."

"What did you do to him?" Eric checked his rifle for damage and flicked the safety on. He let it drop to the end of its strap and looked up.

Hawke drew her dagger and handed it to him, hilt first. The blade had three edges that twisted in a curve around its core to a single point. All three blades were serrated. Their dark colour reflected Werewolf's lights, giving it a dangerous tint.

"Conductive." Hawke said, watching Eric move the curved blade, the light playing across its angles. "Energy blast superheats it."

"And seals the wound," Denthar added.

"And fries out all the fuckin nerves." She smiled cruelly. "And I went right through the spine." Hawke shrugged and looked at the ceiling. "Not that it matters much. Alati soldiers out here in our Rim. I thought he was on the fuckin run from them."

"You know Alatis… It's all about the money." Denthar sighed.

"Yeah. Don't I fuckin know it." Hawke snorted.

The commonroom airlock opened and Bates appeared.

"Enjoy your-fuckin-self?"

Bates grinned, helping Denthar up, while Eric and Hawke climbed to their feet.

"Smooth ride, Captain." Bates took Denthar's rifle from him and led them back into the commonroom. "Charger is meeting us at the alternate rendezvous." He looked back at Hawke and Eric. "Pity the deal went bad. Now what do we do?"

"You'll get fuckin paid." Hawke's growl induced another smile from Bates.

"Expected no less… But did I hear Coni right? They took over the colony?"

"Not our fuckin problem." Hawke sat down heavily in her chair. Her movements were slow as she shrugged out of her jacket and tossed it onto the table. The heavy leather thudded dully.

Eric expected that landing in Werewolf caused more than a few bruises for her. He slipped out of his own jacket and hung it on the back of his chair before sitting.

Hawke poured a large glass of whiskey and slid it to Dent. She looked at Eric and slid a second glass to him, before taking a long swig straight from the bottle.

"Ouch, Nina." Denthar winced while Eric snorted. "Do you have to drink it like that?" He slipped his arm out of its sling and flexed it. "Great, now I don't need it, the Medivi's kick in."

Paladin entered the commonroom and put his guns back in his bag by the table. Charger's third crewmate sat on the couch.

"You are brave." Bates watched Eric sip his drink.

"It is not Martian rum, but it will do."

Denthar's shoulders shook with laughter and he leaned his head on his arms resting on the table.

Hawke leaned back and hooked a leg between the table and her chair. As she cradled the bottle in her lap, she raised the creditdisk to Bates's eye level.

"Never fuckin question, Bates."

He laughed as he took the disk and ran it through a diskreader. He whistled, reading the numbers. "600K, Captains."

Hawke shook her head at Denthar.

"Martians get me every time." Denthar composed himself and sat up. "Did the UTC remove the fear from you when they adapted your ancestors to Mars? Or is it just the way they raised you in that volcano?"

"You know someone from Olympus?"

Denthar nodded. "I grew up on Lunar Terra." Denthar shrugged and lifted his drink. "Did a runner at sixteen to avoid bein recruited into Fleet or FIS. Drifted a bit until I got on the radar of a few people. Then I ended up being introduced to this Ice Bitch over here about five revolutions ago. Been causing trouble ever since."

Eric nodded, taking the information in. He had not met someone out here who knew about his home.

Hawke took a drink. "You've been a pain in my arse ever since."

She looked down as Angel appeared next to her, showing her the screen on a datapad. She ruffled his hair and pointed at the couch.

"Not now."

Unperturbed, he moved over to Denthar and showed him.

"What the?"

"I don't fuckin know." Hawke shrugged. "Kid's up to spatial engineerin or something."

Denthar shook his head and turned back to the boy. "You understand that?"

Angel nodded at Denthar as he sat between the captains.

"Bates, how long till we reach Charger?"

"Couple of hours."

Denthar smiled and relaxed back into his chair. "Ok, give Varsely's disk to Chris. He'll do the split." He looked at Hawke as she inclined her head. "And get the gear stowed."

Bates nodded and went back up the stairs.

"What happens with the Conda4s?" Eric glanced between the pair as they shared a look.

"You thinkin of startin your own mining op out here?" Denthar grinned at Eric's strong headshake. "We sell them. Got more than one contact out here that'll want them and will pay." Denthar looked at Hawke. "You're not wrong, Nina. I might have to spend my time here tryin to convince you to join my crew, Hillar."

Eric looked at Hawke, wondering what she said to the other captain.

She rotated a shoulder, wincing as she worked the muscles.

"I'll give him this, you're fuckin heavy."

Eric smiled, thinking about trying to break her fall in the corridor. "I am what they made me, Captain."

"I'll fuckin drink to that." Hawke raised her bottle and took a big gulp.

Denthar winced and Eric shook his head at her.

"Why do you like Eric so much?" Paladin asked, looking between Denthar and Hawke.

Hawke lowered her bottle and turned to look at Denthar's crew.

Eric felt the air chill as they looked away from her, turning their gaze to the floor.

"Cause, unlike most fuckers out on The Rim, he doesn't suffer from a terminal case of male ego." Hawke raised her bottle to Eric. "Guess that's in the fuckin upbringin too."

"My file?" Eric sipped his drink.

"Martians." Hawke countered.

Eric nodded in understanding. All the comments of her being territorial slipped into place, as did his role in her reactions.

"They knock any toxic masculinity out of you in the mines."

"I don't get it," Paladin said, joining them at the table, while the others found seating on the large couch.

"Mars... The original colony of Mars was female centric." Denthar looked at his glass for a minute. "It made sense. Genetically change your colonisers to breed the next generation efficiently and quickly. It still took cycles to travel between the planets back then."

"I am not following you, Captain."

"All Martians are born female," Eric supplied. "We can choose when and if we want to transfer to another sex when we are older." He shrugged at them. "Not that strange, you know. Lots of animals on Terra did it for centuries before they activated those genes in us."

Eric laughed at the gaping mouths of disbelief on Paladin's and rest of the crews' faces.

"It's just fuckin genetics." Hawke raised her eyes to the ceiling for a long moment. "Get the fuck over it, people."

Denthar shook his head at her.

Eric watched as the rest of them found other more interesting things to discuss over on the couches.

Paladin watched Eric for a moment. "Genetics huh, Captain?" He looked at Hawke. "You seem to know a lot about Martians."

Hawke's bitter laughter had the sharp edge Eric was learning to watch out for.

"Wolf and I are very fuckin good at intelligence mining, Aaron Paladin." Her smile was dark and the colour drained from Paladin's face. "Remember that."

"And you are not exactly afraid of our Ice Pirate Queen, are you, Hillar?" Paladin persisted.

Eric shrugged. "Captain…. You are tough and all that, but when you have faced down three FIS Agents and lived… Killers, do not worry you as much." Eric smiled, while Hawke considered his words for a moment.

"You think I'm worth only three agents?" She looked at Denthar.

Paladin swallowed loudly.

"Not five?" She showed teeth.

"When we are talking agents," Eric dropped the smile as he thought about it, "no. Considering those PAs, I would say you are worth three agents and an Intel."

"See, we've established a basic understandin. Now just hagglin over fuckin value." Hawke chuckled. "I would hope I rate enough for them to send an Enforcer, at the least."

"Maybe…" Eric scratched his goatee. He was enjoying the banter, and Hawke appeared to find it amusing. "But those guys, they can take out entire planets. What do the Alati call him? The Butcher of Sengori. Wiped out the population of a planet. For what? A few high-level Alati councillors." He blinked as Hawke froze for a moment. "Not sure you would rate that high."

"Maybe one rotation, we'll fuckin find out." She took another gulp, then watched the bottle, the liquid swirling.

"You know, The Butcher wasn't so bad." Denthar dismissed the fog that seemed to have gripped the room. "Met him once on Lunar. Drake was his handle… What was his name…?"

"Charlton." Hawke looked up at Denthar.

"That's it." Denthar clicked his fingers. "Alex Charlton. Seemed a decent guy if a bit… I dunno. Something was off with him."

Hawke looked back at the bottle. "The Butcher of Sengori…"

Eric expected that cold, twisted smile but there was nothing.

"Now that would be interestin," Hawke said in a low tone, leaving Eric to wonder if she had forgotten they were there. She lifted the bottle to her lips.

"Well, Hillar, I am sure the captain could find a bunk for you if you want it." Paladin looked at his captain in his attempt to lighten the mood. "We could always use good crewmates."

"What do you think, kid?" Denthar asked Angel, who had been observing the exchange. "Think he'd make a good pirate?"

Angel looked at Eric, then back to Denthar. "He cooks better than you."

Hawke snorted her whiskey while Denthar sat back, looking surprised.

"Makes thirds," Angel added.

"Seriously, kid?" Denthar blinked at Angel.

"So, that was an Alati troop," Eric said, deciding a change of topic was in order.

Denthar sighed. "Despite what Nina might think, we were lucky to get out of there."

He looked at Hawke when she did not react or contradict.

"They can't shoot worth a fuckin damn... But I know that was close, Dent." She shrugged at Eric. "I'm a fuckin realist, get used to it." She looked at Paladin. "You boys are just pirates. Coni, Ana, and me? Well, we are the one thing they can't deal with and would seek to fuckin destroy in any way possible."

Denthar raised his eyebrows at the admission. "Free, uncontrollable women," he said when he saw the confusion on Paladin's face. "That reminds me, didn't you start with a price on your head with the Alatis, Nina? You never told me what you did to deserve that. And the Alati MWLs never state the reason for their bounties."

Hawke surprised them with a shrug. "I was born, Dent." She stood and headed for the stairs. "Don't get fuckin comfortable."

"Born?" Denthar called after her. "You sure about that? I just thought you spun into existence on whiskey and bad choices."

They heard the bitter laugh but to Eric, it sounded tinged with something darker.

"Have not seen her in a good mood like that for a while, Captain." Paladin watched the stairs where Hawke had left.

"She got to fight Fleet, Alatis and start a war with one of the most powerful traders on The Rim in one trip. She's thrilled."

"What did she do to Varsely?"

"Paralysed him, took his money and kept the cargo." Denthar sighed. "She's gonna be ridin the waves of bounty hunters in blood for the next few cycles." He looked at Eric. "You sure you want to stay on Wolf?"

"I am only here for the job." Eric finished his drink and stood, looking at the group over on the couches. Bates had started a poker game. "I'll get something for us to eat."

Angel looked up from his datapad. "Burger?"

Eric adjusted his position on the couch. Coni had loaned him a datapad, and he was reading some files Werewolf allowed him access to. More than once, he had started at the FIS or High-Level Fleet seal, reading about Sirius, Tombstone and Korang. The largest slave operation in the universe and its hunting grounds for stock was in The Rim. The idea chilled his bones and sent his guts churning at the same time. He looked up as Coni walked down the stairs from the bridge.

Hawke was at the mainframe with Chris. The pair were swapping out some circuitboards and wires. Angel was sitting in the mainframe chair, watching. Every so often, Hawke or Chris would show him the part and say something about it. Other than that, the commonroom was quiet. Even the big datascreen near Eric was black instead of running its normal substream news channel.

"I do not know what you and Captain Denthar said to the harbourmaster but he is coming to meet us when we land." Coni leaned against the table while Hawke stood and stretched. Even from the couch, Eric heard the crack. Coni winced at the sound.

"Zeb just wants first chance at the fuckin diggers."

"Word is out on the raid and Varsely." Coni's ears lowered. "You paralysed him from the waist down. He has raised a bonus on you. The bounty hunter to turn you over gets a further 500K from him."

Hawke inclined her head. "For that, I might fuckin turn myself in."

"Captain!"

Hawke grinned at Coni's protest. "Cool it, Con." She shrugged the concern away. "He wouldn't spare you, either. Thinkin about it... I should've gone for the fuckin neck."

Coni ignored the bait, rubbing her head, then scratching an ear.

"And," her purr filled the room with the vibration, "the slave collars at the mining colony failed not long after we left. The mainframe somehow got infected with a virus and the control system crashed."

"Did it?" Hawke moved, reaching for her bottle and tumbler near Coni.

"The colony got their own back on Varsely's men and now have an Alati Corvette to help keep themselves secure."

"Isn't that fuckin something?" Hawke poured a drink and headed for the stairs. She paused at the bottom of them and turned, looking at Coni. "Now, that I would've fuckin paid to watch." She tipped her glass at the Kat and headed up the stairs, Angel following behind her.

Coni's smile was full of teeth when she turned back to Chris and Eric.

Chris finished inserting the last board and closed the mainframe. "Told you she did something with that console." He looked at his sister.

Eric blinked, remembering Hawke leaning against the console, her hand on the jack, the sequence in her commlink light. Eric leaned forward on the couch, putting the datascreen beside him.

"Are you saying she released the colony?" He watched the pair look at each other for a minute.

"I saw a dataline down the connection. I do not know what she did, but it makes sense she sent the mainframe a delayed virus." Chris shrugged, the movement precise and economical. "I do not think it was altruistic. If that Corvette had followed us, we would have been in a mess."

"But... The colony got its freedom back." Coni sighed, sitting in a chair. "She will trust us enough one rotation to tell us, I hope."

"How long have you two been on Wolf?"

"Just over two revolutions." Coni stretched, her tail curling. "It has really only been about one since Jake and Des got their own ships and left. That is when she really opened up a little to us."

"She had to," Chris countered. "Bit hard to raid if you cannot trust the people at your back."

Coni agreed with a nod.

"Jake is Denthar and Des is?"

'Captain Desmond Rowe.' Chris turned to the mainframe and brought up the images of the two ships.

Eric recognised Charger. The other one was a little bigger but had that modern streamlined look and gun turrets he would expect for a ship that might see combat.

"That is Resolute."

Both were Terran designed. Eric recognised the three engines in triangular formation at the rear and the single axis design.

"Nice." Eric focused on the guns, comparing them to the rifles of Werewolf. The other two pirate ships had larger guns and were mounted on 360 turrets, covering every angle a ship could come at them. "They certainly look the part."

"Of a pirate ship?" Chris smiled and glanced at Eric before turning back to the screen. His tail swung. "Wolf hides her nature. We have the advantage that we can land anywhere in Terran space with the right passes, and no one would look at her twice. She is just an old beaten-up hauler. Only problem is when the captain walks out of the ship."

Coni purred at the thought.

Eric sat back, giving the pair a fresh look.

Chris was a cyborg type that had been common in the asteroid mines and the shipyards about 300 revolutions ago. His entire body, except the brain and part of his spine, was completely metal, with gears and circuits. He was stronger and faster than a natural-bodied Kat. Except for the hidden gun holster, he was a more standard-body replacement for a civilian than outfitted for battle.

Coni was smaller than her bother, but that might have just been because Chris's cybernetic body was older, bulkier technology. She was completely natural and never carried a gun. Eric was not even sure if she knew how to use one, although he remembered her being handy with those claws on Sirius.

"I must admit, you two do not exactly fit my idea of pirates either."

"You could say that we fell into it." Coni's eyes dilated and she laughed.

"Fell?" Eric blinked, not understanding.

"Our owner made a terrible choice of words when dealing with Hawke." Chris shrugged again. "Con tried to warn him, but he never listened. Why he bothered owning an empath and never took notice of her, I do not know."

"Owner?" Eric blinked. "You were slaves?" He focused more intently on the Kats, letting the rest of Chris's words sink in. "You are an empath, Coni?"

"The fur has never really grown in properly," Coni muttered, touching the back of her neck. "Even after those revolutions out of the collar." She dropped her paw and shrugged. "I do not advertise I am an empath. Too many people try to take advantage. Besides, I can barely control it. Captain says I will improve, but the collar stopped me developing my skills. It is not worth the hassle in others knowing."

"And Hawke freed you?"

"Another non-altruistic event." Chris laughed. "She got sick of hints of cheaper rates if she proved she was a woman. She decked our owner and shoved him into a crate that was probably too small to fit him. Denthar then offered us a ride to Tombstone."

"But... they had a few stops on the way and eventually we settled in here and did not want the ride." Coni leaned back in her chair. "What about you, Eric?"

"About me?" Eric felt his guts clench, realising what she was asking.

"Hawke likes you," Coni replied. "We have had none of the usual grumbling or threats to throw you out of an airlock. Even Captain Denthar said you were good in a fight."

"Did not run from those PAs either." Chris chimed in.

"Would you consider going full-time pirate?" Coni watched him as he thought about it.

"To be honest, this is not where I thought I would end up." Eric looked at his hands, rubbing that scar on his wrist. "My life was all planned out for me on Mars. Work the mines, raise my girls, and grow old and grumpy when the cycle-long storms cover the settlement."

Coni purred as he laughed bitterly.

"My eldest died in a mining accident. They should not have reopened the old tunnels, but the UTC quotas were higher than ever, and we had not even reached the last revolution's take yet. I tried to stay out of the unrest, but..."

"You never could stay out of trouble." Coni finished for him.

Eric nodded. "After her death, more tunnels collapsed. We were talking at the tribal council. We refused to mine anymore until the UTC delivered on the safety equipment they had promised us." He shrugged. "Before any of us really knew it, it had escalated into Fleet troops being sent to oversee the production, and FIS trying to infiltrate and control. You would think after generations of it, Mars would no longer have the fight left in them. We proved them wrong."

"So, what happened?" Chris looked at the mainframe. "Details are pretty sketchy out here."

"What was always going to happen. There was no way the UTC would let Mars out of their control. Not the nearest planet to Terra. It was almost like the whole thing was a setup from the start. Create an uprising, then destroy it as an example to everyone else."

Eric showed them the scar on his wrist. "I escaped the cells. Fought through three FIS agents on Titan and paid my way onto a cargoship headed out of the Sol system." He dropped his hand. "Did not know about the terrorist line until I made it to the borderstation. By then, I had slipped off the radar and was working my way out here as a manual labourer."

"And now?" Coni prompted after a long silence.

"I do not know," Eric admitted. "I did not think past getting out here, away from the UTC and I do not see Hawke dropping off their radar soon. Not sure I want to be standing near her when they decide to take matters seriously."

"Good point." Coni's ears lowered. "I do not think she will be happy until she is number one on their MWLs." She shook her head. "It is like she wants that attention."

Eric remembered Hawke's comment to him about that. He smiled. "Giving them her own brand of fuck you." He looked at the datascreen again. "Why Denthar? Why not call him Jake?"

Chris shrugged. "Some joke between them. She says she does not like the name."

Chris shrugged. "Some joke between them. She says she does not like the name."

"Wait." Coni stared at Eric, her ears forward, whiskers quivering. "You said 'girls'. You left your family back on Mars?"

"I..." Eric's shoulders tensed. A flood of pain and loss conflicted with rage within him.

Coni and Chris shared a look. Their Kat ears twisted as the pair communicated without words.

Eric exhaled. His shoulders dropped as he let the feelings pass.

"Sorry." He shook his head, clearing the last of the anger. "I did. My youngest, Sophie. Her mother, Annette, took her to a mining complex at Sol's asteroid belt." He spoke rest in a rush. "There was an implosion. No one survived."

"I am sorry, Eric." Coni's whiskers drooped.

Eric attempted a smile, but it felt hollow.

#

Eric dug the Sirius map out of his bag and climbed the stairs from the lower level. He shoved it into his jacket pocket and hitched his backpack over his shoulder.

As he looked up, he found Hawke watching him from her seat at the commonroom table. She held out a creditdisk. Coni and Angel were sitting on the couch, looking at something on their datapads. He walked over to the captain and grinned, noticing her gunbelt and jacket were on.

"Expecting trouble?" He eyed the jacket again as he took the disk. "That thing must be seriously armoured."

"It does its job." Hawke shrugged. "That's your share." She nodded towards the disk in Eric's hand.

"I never asked what the deal was." He dropped his bag on the table, unzipped it and dug a hand into it to find his creditreader.

"Half always to the ship first." Hawke pulled out her gun and checked the battery life. "The crew gets the rest, even split."

Pulling the creditreader out, Eric turned it on and inserted the disk. "Sounds fair."

He trailed off as the numbers flashed across his screen: *80,000.* Eric blinked. The number did not register for a minute. A quick sum in his head translated it back to UTC credits. He shook his head, realising it was more than his tribe's mining quota for a sequence.

"Includin a bonus."

Eric looked up at Hawke as she stood. "You needed that generator."

"He picks things up quick." Coni looked up from her spot on the couch, putting the datapad down. Eric glanced at her.

"Noticed that." Hawke appeared to be continuing a conversation. "What do you think, kid?" Hawke was watching Eric as she spoke.

Angel looked up from his datapad. "He makes good burgers."

Coni purred and Hawke looked at the ceiling for a moment.

"That kid'll be the fuckin death of me." She looked back at Eric. "My advice: leave your gear here. Take only a few cred. We're docked for three rotations. You've that long to decide." She turned and headed for the rear airlock.

Eric watched the doors shut behind her.

"Was I just offered a job?" He looked at Coni, who showed a full row of teeth with her smile.

"I will get you a clean creditdisk. I think 500 should do it."

Angel resettled his datapad on his lap and lifted a hand to his commlink. He tapped it on with a finger. "Coolios."

0.17

Eric leaned against Rebeal's bar. The metal counter steadied him as his heart rate slowed. He flexed his fingers along the cool surface. Hawke laughed as she leaned past him to swipe her creditdisk into the reader.

"You get used to her driving." Chris patted Eric on the shoulder. He turned to the far corner of the bar. "Captain, that new trader, Gegor, is here. He should have what we need."

"The Ant?" Hawke nodded at the bar's owner. "Can deal with him. Set it up."

Chris disappeared into Rebeal's crowd.

"Bob, usual for us." She looked at Eric. "Get him some Mons rum... Looks like he fuckin needs it."

The Custurian gurgled as he put a full glass of whiskey on the bench before reaching for another tumbler.

"They do not listen... as usual. Will destroy my bar in the process." Bob looked at Eric, then back to Hawke.

Hawke shrugged and she picked her drink up. "They pay the fuckin damages." She looked behind them towards the stairs and waited.

A few minutes later, Chris slipped in between her and Eric, and took the drink left for him.

"All set."

"You not deal with them now?" The Custurian blinked his multiple eyelids.

Hawke's icy laughter filtered across the bar.

"Business first, Bob. Then pleasure." She inclined her head to Eric and she inhaled. "Don't get me fuckin wrong, you're a piece of work, Mr Hillar... But I don't care for the fuckin hormones."

Eric opened his mouth, confused, but paused as he felt the familiar tail wrap around his thigh. He smiled, glancing at Kei, the hormones filled his nose.

"Thanks, Captain." Kei's arm slid around Eric's while he reached for the glass of rum with the other hand. "I am not a fan of your style of fun, either."

"You should try it." Hawke tipped her glass at Bob. "You might find you fuckin enjoy it."

"And I maintain you might enjoy it my way." Kei countered. "Got some straps and chains if you ever get curious."

Eric froze, expecting an angry response from Hawke.

"I'm not Coni." Hawke flicked her hand in a dismissive motion.

Eric blinked and glanced between them, his guts churning with the thought he was missing something.

Hawke watched him.

Eric groaned, realising what Hawke implied about Coni… and Kei. He flushed and his pants felt uncomfortably tight. He swallowed hard.

"Just be sure to remind people you've no fuckin clue about space mechanics, Mr Hillar."

"Huh?" Eric watched Hawke walk away. "Space…? Wait, is that why you picked me?" Eric's gut now twisted.

Hawke turned to look at him. Her mouth curved into that dark smile.

"You knew I would not understand how Werewolf worked." He said this loud enough to start murmurs from the patrons near them.

"You never fuckin asked, Mr Hillar." Hawke chuckled. She motioned to Chris and the pair moved towards the far corner of the room, under the mezzanines.

Around Eric and Kei, the muttering grew.

"I…" Eric looked at Kei, unsure why Hawke had said that.

"Told you to be careful. You were on her ship for nearly three cycles." Kei raised an eyebrow. "Many people would give a limb for that chance, just to see what makes her ship tick."

"From what I saw, whiskey and bad choices." Eric rolled his eyes at the thought of the PAs. "About my name…"

Kei shrugged. "I like it better than Jon."

Eric exhaled. Kei smiled at him as he lifted the rum to his lips.

He blinked, realising it was a decent and rather expensive drop. The spices were balanced just right and the rum warmed his throat perfectly. He looked at the Custurian, whose tentacles wiggled with laughter.

"She only gets the best for the crew." Eric looked at the shadows near the stairs. The word 'crew' rebounded in his thoughts. He shook his head, trying to figure out Hawke's intentions. "Pity the standard they catch her. She appreciates the elixir."

"I figure she has a lot more to destroy before then." Kei pulled on Eric's arm. "Come on. I still have a few of your things."

Eric glanced back at the mezzanines before they headed for the storage door. The shadows felt more populated than usual to him, the general noise of the bar subdued. Hawke seemed oblivious to it. She was talking to a gigantic creature. Its body was covered in a dark grey exoskeleton with eight limbs. It was using four of them as arms as it spoke.

The doors in front of Eric and Kei opened to let a few of the serving staff through. A couple of them turned and waved at him before heading off to their destination. Eric and Kei slipped into the storage rooms once they passed.

"I take it you are collecting your things." Sasha's voice was loud in the large, dark storage space. She stood in the doorway to the kitchen. Behind her were the familiar sounds of the team talking, laughing, the clatter of dishes and the bubbling of cooking.

"Chef."

"You tore that apron." Sasha crossed her arms.

Eric considered his options for a moment. "I am sorry. I can pay for it."

She watched him, processing his words, her expression sceptical. "I have taken it out of your wages."

"No argument there." He ran his hand over his scalp and down his face in a gesture of respect. "I am sorry I could not live up to your expectations, Chef." He glanced at the closed doors to the bar and the slow murmur he could hear through it.

"I think you did," Sasha contradicted him, handing over a creditdisk. She smiled slightly. "Just not the ones I was hoping you would."

Kei pulled on his arm. Eric motioned farewell to Sasha and let Kei direct him towards the commonroom.

"I thought you had packed all my things."

She slid her arm under his jacket. Her expression was thoughtful as she felt the gun in its holster and the spare batteries hanging on the other side.

"I did." She smiled as he rested his arm over her shoulders. "But if I take you to the service rooms, I will have to charge."

"Never paid for it before." Eric breathed in the cloud of hormones surrounding him again.

Kei nuzzled his ear as they reached the stairwell. She looked up the stairs, then back at him. With a smile, she slipped her fingers down his pants and around his shaft.

"Keep doing that..." he swallowed, finding a wall to rest her against, "and I will not make it..." He kissed her neck and moved steadily down while she continued stroking him long and soft.

Her little gasping noises encouraged him to keep moving his hands along her thighs and up under the skirt of her dress. Finding her pantie-less and warm drove a groan out of him.

"Here, now." Kei moaned in his ear, working the buckle of his pants.

Eric felt the rim on his underwear being tugged down. His penis swelled as she pulled it out. Lifting Kei up against the wall, he carefully slid into her, feeling her cooling sensation. She matched his intention to take it slow, moaning low in his ear, the sound in sync with his slow insertion.

Eric used the wall behind Kei to hold her, his hips thrusting harder and faster. The steady thump of their movements echoed along the wall, making their attempts to muffle grunts, squeals and groans useless.

Kei clenched her legs against his thighs, her belly quivering as she came, breathing hard and shaking.

Eric grinned and pushed again and again. Holding on as long as he could, he let her crest turn into shivers and moans of pleasure until he finally shuddered. His shoulders shook half with laughter, half with effort as they slowed and stopped. He put his hand against the wall to take the weight from his shaking legs.

Seizing an opportunity, Kei licked the salty sweat from his throat.

"That—"

The click of a safety and the sound of an energy gun powering up silenced Eric.

They froze.

"Both hands on the wall, Hillar."

Eric sat against the cold metal wall, his knees bunched up, arms resting on them. Around him, the space was divided into two. The cell he was in had an electronic barrier, locking him off from the other side of the room. A single door was on the far wall opposite him. A camera sat on its mount above the doorframe, its iris periodically scanning the space. The lights above him flickered and buzzed. He occasionally got the faint smell of burning wire.

The door opened. He looked up, watching a large form step into the space. The blue tinge of the energy barrier between him and the cyborg, made its metal body glint with cold light. The tall frame was heavily armoured. Blue paintwork in the design of swirls and waves covered one shoulder, before disappearing under the body it was carrying.

Eric recognised the cyborg as Grong. He had seen him a few times in Rebeal but had kept his distance, not trusting that the sanctity of the bar would keep him safe from the price on his head.

Hawke hung from Grong's shoulder. Her ponytail almost dragged on the grillwork floor behind them.

Grong glanced at Eric as the front of the cell deactivated.

Eric did not move.

The cyborg dumped Hawke face down on the floor. She barely stirred, appearing to be unconscious. Wordlessly, Grong turned, reactivated the barrier and left the room. The lock clicked the door shut.

Eric scrambled over to her. There was a hole in the armoured jacket at her spine, exposing black and red skin. Spreading from the black burn, blisters raised into lumps of milky white. The leather at the edge of the hole was singed and smoked a little. He recognised the acidic taint of cooked meat.

He reached for her shoulder but paused, unsure if he would hurt her more or if she would react badly to the touch.

"Are you still breathing?" he asked in Trade. For a moment, Eric wondered if Hawke knew Trade. He was fairly certain she would not understand Martian. If she did not know it, communicating without their commlinks was going to be complicated.

"Course I am fucking breathing." Breathless, Hawke's voice cracked with effort from speaking. Despite this, her Trade was flawless to Eric's ears.

She moved her arms slowly, getting them under her. As she rolled over onto her back, her legs twitched. With a grimace, she raised a knee and lifted her hips to get a heel under her arse. Her expression eased a little as she lifted the weight off her lower back. The rest of her body remained sprawled across the floor.

"He would not last long if he killed every alive-only bounty he went for." Hawke smiled coldly before covering her eyes with her arm and exhaled loudly. Her other hand rested on her chest. "Fucker blind-sighted me." Her tone betrayed a small amount of admiration for the feat.

Eric smiled and sat back against the wall.

"Is that even possible?" He leaned his head against the cool metal.

Hawke chuckled. She lifted her arm from her eyes to look at him. Her gaze then flickered to the camera above the door. The arm dropped again over her face, her watch dangling loose on her wrist from its half-opened clasp.

"So far, the evidence suggests it fucking is." She growled adjusting her waist.

"You can move your legs at least."

"Fucker set the cannon high enough to scramble the nerves but not to fuck me up completely. Where are we?"

"Not sure." Eric followed her gaze and watched the camera as it rotated slowly across the room. "They put me in a transport. Not even sure we are still on Sirius."

"We are." The arm left her face, and fingers spread across the floor as she laid it out straight. "Feel that? It is Sirius's engines."

Eric dropped a hand to the cool metal floor and felt the tiniest vibration. "Do you know if Kei is safe?"

Hawke snickered. "Never underestimate that woman's ability with those nails of hers."

He laughed in relief. "One rotation, I will learn to stop worrying about her."

"If you can help it, never stop that." Her smile was not as cold now. "She is capable with those throwers of hers, but no one is above concern."

"Throwers?" Eric's stomach tightened at the word. "As in, throwing daggers?"

"She burned her cover getting away from those dicks and reaching Dent. You might as well know."

"Always thought she was too familiar with you and the others."

At first, anger flashed through his thoughts but almost immediately Eric let the feeling go. He has never asked Kei about her past or the reasons she had been a grillworker with Rebeal. He had merely accepted and taken what she offered.

"And... I did always think my first standard on Sirius was a little too easy."

"You got that job in the kitchen on your own." That snarky contempt was back in Hawke's tone, but her smile remained unchanged. "And fucking unexpected."

Eric smiled in return. After a few moments, he exhaled and leaned against the cold wall. "Why did you say that in the bar? The thing about space mechanics?"

"Everyone wants a fucking piece." Hawke's sigh was more of a pained grunt than anything else. "And you don't have the fucking protection of being known as one of the Brethren—yet."

Eric chuckled. He stretched his neck, resting the back of his skull on the wall and looked up at the ceiling. Thoughts of what might await them on their return to the UTC were not pleasant.

"I never really thought much about what I would do out here. But I was not expecting it to be this short."

"I am not having my fucking arse paraded in front of those fucking UTC news reporters. That is for fucking sure."

Eric smiled and he looked back at Hawke. "I do not think you would have much choice about that."

She made a tiny shift of her arm, staring at him. Her eyes glowed under the shadows. "Although it could make for an interesting fucking bulletin."

She snorted and Eric shook his head in disbelief at her amusement.

"Who knows, make enough datastreams and your daughter might find out you are still breathing."

Eric froze, cold leeching through his jacket and into his back. His chest ached.

"My girls are dead."

"What?" Hawke angled her chin slightly, looking at him. With a humph, she resettled the arm. "Wondered why you ran solo."

Her words echoed through Eric's mind. He swallowed, staring at her.

"Let me fucking guess: they implied she had died with your wife?"

"I…"

"Fucking figures."

The mixture of disbelief, relief and bitter regret froze his lungs.

"But I saw the FIS file. My girl, Josie, was killed when the mining station on Pallas had a blowout. Annette deserved that but not my little Josie."

"Never trust a FIS file. Particularly one left where you can access it." Hawke's tone had that assumption of command. "Now, Mr Hillar, you have run out of time. I need a fucking answer."

Eric swallowed. "I… I have to go—"

"Back?"

Eric blinked at her bitter laugh.

"That is exactly what they want you to fucking try."

Eric thought he heard something in her tone, a combination of temptation and regret. His eyes narrowed.

"Your only fucking hope is making enough noise out here to get your girl's attention."

Something clicked in Eric's mind, a conversation on Werewolf when he and Hawke stared at the starlines.

"My own special brand of 'fuck you'?"

Hawke graced him with that dark grin again.

"What did you leave behind, Captain?"

"Bad memories and a fucking mess. Give me a fucking answer."

"Yes." The word left Eric's lips before he realised the decision was made. His shoulders relaxed.

Truthfully, he had decided a while ago. That moment in the stairwell at the colony. Hawke pushed Denthar out of harm's way and gave Eric time to move. The way she had protected them from the expulsion into space. The way the Kats trusted Hawke, even though no one seemed to know a thing about her from before she arrived on The Rim. She drew people to her, like Denthar. And, then there was the boy…

Hawke raised the hand from her chest and flicked it. A long, thin dart slid through the energy barrier and hit the iris of the camera. There was a small flicker of energy, and its indicator light blinked orange at them.

"A FIS dart?" Eric climbed to a crouch, watching the camera before turning back to Hawke, who was fiddling with her jacket. "How did you get one of those?"

"FIS Enforcer." She raised her eyebrows at him. "Same place I got this." She raised her hand again and twirled a small thin rod through her fingers. "I take it you know where to fucking stick it?"

Eric felt a slow grin spread across his face. "It is not my first time."

He moved forward and took the outstretched pick, then crouched next to the energy barrier, searching for the tiny nodes of the reed point that would disable the whole thing. He chuckled, hearing Hawke's quiet laughter.

"You met an Enforcer and lived?" Eric realised, disbelief colouring his tone.

She snorted. "And their whole fucking team."

Eric glanced at Hawke. She watched him from under her arm again.

"Enforcers never work alone, do not forget that. That is why they are so fucking dangerous. And hurry the fuck up. Grong will notice the loop in the camera feed soon."

"I know." Eric slid along the edge of the barrier, looking down at the channel. "Do not think I would ever rate high enough for FIS sending an Enforcer after me though."

"Never know." Her voice had that amused tint again.

Eric grunted in disbelief. He found the spot. He slid the rod carefully between the nodes to close the circuit. The energy barrier powered down.

"Come on." He scrambled to his feet, moving over to the door. He checked the control panel next to it. Its indicator lights were a solid green: *locked*. He heard Hawke muttering behind him in an unfamiliar language. The tone and harshness revealed her words to be curses.

"Hillar."

He turned at the unguarded tone in her voice.

She had reached her knees but seemed unable to stand. "Need your shoulder."

"You are accepting help now, Captain?" Eric smiled, crouching beside her. She gave him that same expressionless look she had given Denthar's crew. He laughed.

She snorted and gripped his shoulder.

"Ready?" Eric grabbed her elbow and stood. They grunted into a standing position.

"Fuck—fucking—," she growled as he straightened slowly, giving her time to balance her weight and steady the shake in her legs. 'Fuck.'

He winced as her grip tightened. The force of it threatened to crush his shoulder bone.

"Can you walk?"

"Only one fucking way to find out," Hawke snarled, one foot sliding across the floor. She put her weight on it and moved her second foot, lifting it a little.

Eric kept pace with her until they reached the door and the control panel. "Got any ideas?"

Hawke let his shoulder go to lean against the wall. She glanced at the control panel.

"Can you reach the dart?" She looked up at the camera.

"It is a stretch, but I can." Eric glanced at it. "The minute I do though, they will see we are out."

"Get my pick and the dart, then get ready." Hawke pointed at the other side of the door, then went back to looking at the control panel. She re-clasped the links of her watch. The zeros blinked on the watch's face but did not update.

Eric collected the pick and reached up to pull the dart loose.

Hawke moved to the edge of the door. Beside her, the control panel blinked: *unlocked.*

Eric handed her the tools and moved to where she had directed. He watched her slip the items into a hidden spot under the metal patch on her shoulder.

"You—"

She raised a finger to hush him and turned her head to listen.

He copied her position against the opposite doorframe, only just hearing a murmur through the thick metal.

Hawke lifted a second finger, and a third. She then dropped the third back down. There was a ping as the control panel signalled the door was opening.

Two men walked through the door. Eric grabbed the forearm of the one nearest to him. He dragged the hunter against him, placing him in a headlock. Next, Eric lifted him high off the ground, squeezed and twisted. There was a crack and he felt the man's neck break. He snapped the shoulder strap of the corpse's rifle, freeing the weapon quickly. Setting it against his shoulder, Eric readied the weapon.

Hawke slammed the other hunter into the doorframe. His nose caved into his skull. Blood spattered across the metal and across her cheek. She pulled the handgun out of the hunter's hip holster, letting his body drop to the floor with a thud. She glowered at the simple-looking design of the weapon and flicked the safety off.

"Fucking cheap, plastic knockoffs." She looked at Eric. "Need to find our gear."

"Not enough spares in that hangar crate?" He checked the corridor, trying to hide the smile as she glanced at him, her expression dark.

"I need my fucking gear." Hawke used the doorframe to help step over the body and move into the corridor.

Eric blinked at the bloody imprints from Hawke's fingers that smeared along the wall.

He followed her to the corridor, checking both ways before focusing on the captain. Looking at the state of her back wound, the image of her in the mining colony, leaning against the console, came to his mind. He thought about those pins and needles he had felt at her contact when they had jumped into space. How it had felt like an electronic airlock does on your skin when passing through it. Her unaccountable weight, speed, strength...

"You are a Cina," Eric blurted.

Hawke stopped and turned slightly to look at him.

Eric stared back. The propaganda from the UTC came unbidden to his mind. Capable of linking with computers, controlling energy in any electronics, Cinas were the strength of the Fleet's battleships, with their ability to link with the mainframes and add flexibility to their programming... and their weakness.

"The kid is too." He flushed hot, expecting denial or anger from her.

Hawke's head angled, watching him like the predator she was named after.

"I thought the UTC had your kind all locked up or regulated."

"Just like all Martians never leave their mines?" she countered, her tone controlled.

Eric thought she was now weighing his acceptance of joining the crew against his sudden realisation. He breathed when her gun did not turn towards him. He could still smell the burn of the blast she had taken. The stench of cooked leather and meat radiated from her.

"He tried to paralyse you."

Hawke shrugged noncommittally.

"Grong does not know what you are. Can you fry him?"

Hawke smiled at that. She started down the corridor again, gun ready.

"See... That is the right way to think." She reached a t-intersection, checked it was empty, then looked up at the ceiling.

Eric saw the glow in her eyes and now recognised it for what it was: Hawke was looking at the energy and datalines in the walls to find a way out.

"Turn everything to your advantage, Mr Hillar." She took a few steps and turned right into a new corridor. She pointed at a nearby door. "That one."

Eric moved forward, reaching the door well ahead of her. He could hear movement from the other side but no voice. The corridor ended with three more doors only metres from Eric. They all stood open, showing crates and equipment, most covered in storage film.

Hawke reached the door and listened for a moment. She nodded at him, showing him a single finger.

With a smile, Eric kicked the door open and pointed his rifle into the room. He killed the hunter before she had even stood from her chair. He slipped into the room and looked around, Hawke close behind him.

Eric moved to another door in the space. It opened to an equipment room. Their gear sat piled on a small bench near the door.

There was a thump. Eric looked back into the other room.

Hawke had pushed the woman off the seat and leaned against the console. She was looking at the datascreen. An image of their cell room was static. At the bottom of the screen, a hand from one of the dead hunters and a pool of blood came into view as the camera turned.

Eric turned back to the equipment room, slung two rifles over his shoulder, and gathered their gear. When he returned to the console, he found Hawke watching him.

He put the thick, coiled loops of leather and hard carbon-based canisters of her gunbelt next to her and rested one rifle against the console.

She adjusted the belt on the table to reach for a container, pulling out a small tube before she held it up between them. With a flick of a button on the side, a long, thin syringe shot out of it.

"In the spine." She reset the device, the syringe disappearing again and held it out to Eric. "As close to the centre of the damage as you can get."

He put his gunbelt and rifle down and took the canister. It looked like a simple metal tube, cold in his hand and completely inert.

"Painkiller?" He stepped around her, getting the wound into view again.

The blisters had reduced a little, their sacks sagging as the liquid inside drained away. Even her red-raw skin had lightened, but the black hole was still dark and burnt looking. He gritted his teeth, wondering just how much pain she was enduring to move.

"Coni Cocktail: pains, Medivi and a pile of other shit she says is good for healing."

"Is there anything you don't have in those containers?" Eric set the canister in his hand and looked for the right spot to place it.

"Patience for fucks who think they can claim my bounty."

Eric chuckled. "Ready?"

"Do it," she snarled.

Eric pressed the syringe against her spine, triggering the needle. He heard the hiss of the injection firing. Hawke's shoulders tensed, then relaxed, as he gently pulled the needle out and clicked it back into the canister. He watched the black of the wound lighten, and the red ease towards an angry pink. Even the blisters shrank back into her skin. He handed back the canister.

Hawke shoved it into her gunbelt, before digging into another container and pulling out a commlink. As she fitted it to her ear, it blinked the start-up sequence.

Eric found his own commlink in the pile of gear and put it in his ear. The pings warning him that there was no external connection.

"That's fuckin better." Hawke immediately stopped speaking with Trade.

He smiled, putting his side holster on. Drawing his gun, he checked the battery: *100%*.

There was a clatter as Hawke took her own gunbelt off the console and started clipping it on.

"What happened to Werewolf?"

The clinking stopped. Hawke looked up from her thigh straps.

"Her mainframe is shutdown." She finished adjusting her straps and drew her gun, looking at the indicator as she flicked it on. "In the middle of installin the generator." She checked her other gun. "They've interfered with our long-distance comms. Chris was told to bring Des and Dent if he didn't clear the blackout in an hour."

"So, either they cannot fix it or it has not been an hour yet."

Hawke shrugged in answer. She reached for her dagger at the back of her gunbelt, her arm not stretching enough to retrieve it. Trying again, she spat a curse when she could not get her hand around the grip and picked up the rifle. She checked its setting and battery, before settling it against the crook of her arm.

"This console is fuckin useless. Closed circuit for the cells only. No connection to Sirius's network." She winced but stood on her own. "No cameras outside of the cell." She started walking toward the corridor. "This isn't his primary base. They'd be more gear if it was."

Eric grabbed his rifle and followed.

"Pretty empty, too. Where is everyone?"

"Attemptin to complete the bounty." She returned to the t-intersection, checking it before nodding to Eric it was clear.

"Complete the bounty?"

"Wolf." She turned, looking at him for a moment, then snorted, amused. "If they convince the harbourmaster to tell them where she is, Wolf can hold her own... Even without the mainframe."

She started down the corridor.

"Your bounty is for the ship too. I forgot about that." Eric passed her and stopped at the intersection, checking the way to the cell room and the other corridor. "Why is that?" He looked back at her when silence followed his question.

Hawke stopped where the corridors met and was looking at the cell door at the end. The bodies of the two hunters they had killed were visible in the doorway.

"Who did you steal her from?"

"She's mine." Hawke's tone was metal. She turned back to him, eyes hard. "I'll steal anything that'll make me a profit, Mr Hillar, but never fuckin forget this: Wolf is mine."

Her gaze returned to the cell door and the force left her words. "That's the fuckin problem. They want what's mine." She almost stepped back towards the cell, then turned and headed the other way. "One of them had a fuckin dead-man alarm. Grong knows we're out."

Eric waited for her to reach him before moving again. "The Kats do not know about you, do they?"

There was a loud exhale. "They're Korang born and bred. Don't even fuckin know their own history. Not that there's much of it. They're older, but the fuckin kid's seen more than them." She growled, then sighed. "No. Chris knows what I can do, but not how or why."

"Coni?" Eric checked the next door. The storeroom was empty. They moved forward again.

"The lovesick empath." She rolled her eyes. "She's got no fuckin idea. Just thinks if I find someone, I'll suddenly get more... Terran."

Eric stopped and stared at her, hearing her frustration edged with something. Something that sounded a lot like loneliness.

"How old are you?"

She shook her head. "You lose track of time in The Rim."

For a moment, he thought she was dodging the question, but she looked thoughtful, not stubborn.

"Sixty... I think. Maybe sixty-one revolutions."

"A few less than me." Eric smiled and she shrugged. "Denthar is what? Mid-twenties?"

"Something like that... These questions have a fuckin point?"

"And I was buying into the killer." Eric chuckled. "How long has it been since you had someone you could talk to?"

"I also kill, Mr Hillar."

There was a threat in her tone, but Eric did not feel that she was directing it at him.

"Thought I was crew?"

Hawke inclined her head a little and turned to check inside the next room.

"Fuckin dead. Not a single computer or comms setup. For a cyborg, he's runnin his specs low."

"You said this was not his primary base. The active equipment is probably somewhere else."

Eric checked the room on his right. It was full of bunk beds. The next room was a bathroom, dark and empty.

"Or he has figured out what you are and is keeping you away from his network."

She raised her eyebrows.

They moved slowly past more doors, all sleeping quarters. The last door opened into a commonroom. They had fitted the space with a lounge, a table and, in the corner, a small kitchen.

Eric glanced at the large double doors opposite them. Their control panel lit by a solid green: *locked*.

Hawke entered the room and leaned against the table. There was a slight shake in her arms as she moved before resting on the metal counter. Her rifle pointed at the double doors with a low aim. Sweat made the hair under her ponytail dark and her feather tattoos glisten.

"You up for what is about to come?"

"Mr Hillar." She fixed him with that dangerous look again. "You get some fuckin leeway but never fuckin ask me again if I'm up for a fight." There was a slight edge to her lips, that tiny almost non-existent smile.

Eric felt the adrenaline rise as her rifle raised higher towards the doors.

"You going to kill Grong for this?"

"I won't kill him." She shook her head. "I'm gonna fry every fuckin circuit in his body. I'm gonna melt every fuckin wire through his systems. I'm gonna burn every fuckin connection to his brain and leave the fuck driftin in blackness for eternity."

The door panel flickered to red. Eric raised his rifle but held off firing when Hawke did not move.

Grong stepped into the room, doors closing behind. His arm was unnaturally straight, his hand hanging on a hinge. He raised it towards Hawke, exposing the cannon underneath the hand at her.

Hawke only raised her eyebrow at him.

Eric adjusted his rifle, waiting for Hawke's lead.

She did not move. She just watched Grong.

"I have the right setting this time... Hawke." Grong said.

"I know how to see you comin now."

"That will not help you on a UTC penal planet." Grong glanced at Eric before indicating her rifle with his cannon. "We will survive a blast from this, but would he?" He stepped forward. "Drop the guns."

Eric held his breath. Hawke glanced at him before she looked at her rifle. There was a tense few seconds where he wondered what she would do, then she flicked the rifle off. His heart sank. She lowered it carefully to the table and slid it out of easy reach.

"Handguns too."

They followed the rifle.

"Now." Grong looked at Eric and stepped towards him. "Your turn."

Eric's finger tensed on the trigger. He stared as Grong stepped closer, the cyborg turning his back to Hawke, blocking Eric's view of her.

There was a scrambling sound.

Hawke's arm appeared, wrapping around Grong's neck. She pulled herself up to the cyborg's shoulders. Her other arm lifted, the dagger in her hand.

Grong straightened, gears whirring loudly as he reached for her. The sound of mechanics grinding filled the space.

"Never fuckin turn your back." Hawke stabbed her dagger into the jacks in the back of the cyborg's neck. "Get down."

Letting go of the dagger, she reached forward. Catching Grong's cannon arm, she yanked it up.

The urgency in Hawke's voice surprised Eric enough to obey without question. He dove to the floor, the cannon fire hitting the ceiling behind him. He felt heat from the energy blast, even from the floor. He got to his feet, crouching, and brought his rifle around.

Energy crackled across Grong's and Hawke's shoulders as she regripped the dagger. Eric's eyes ached from the intensity of the light.

The crunching and crushing of gears seizing in Grong's body tore through the surrounding air. The cyborg grunted. The speaker in his voice box squealed, then descended into an irregular tick.

Hawke growled, eyes shining as she forced the dagger in further, twisting it.

"You… fuck." Energy surged down her blade.

Grong's eyes froze, then burned out. The black pits smoked and he crashed facedown to the floor, Hawke landing on top of him. She snarled, pulling the dagger free.

He stood slowly, watching Hawke as she straightened and motioned to sheath her weapon.

"For fuck's sake." Her back shook as muscles seized. The dagger clattered to the floor.

"Captain?" Eric breathed.

Hawke focused on her hand, flexing the fingers. She looked up at Eric as he moved closer to her. She snorted.

"Did not expect that." Eric held out a hand for her.

"Neither did this fuck." She flicked the back of Grong's skull with her fingers. There was a dull metal twang.

"No, I mean, you sounded concerned for me."

She ran her hand over her head and down her ponytail, before looking up at the ceiling. She exhaled slowly, then looked at him.

"I'm only gonna say this fuckin once." Hawke fixed him with that same dark look she had when she spoke earlier of Werewolf. "If you can't trust or be trusted, you leave the second we are out of this fuckin mess."

Eric swallowed, feeling the blood drain from his face. "Even though I know what you are?"

She snorted again, then winced as she struggled to her feet, ignoring his offered hand. "I don't hide what I am. I just don't parade it the fuck around."

"Denthar knows?"

She nodded, looking down at the blade on the floor.

Eric could see the thought clearly, as if she said it aloud: she was unsure she could pick it up. He bent down to collect it. He marvelled again at the glint of the dark blade in his hand, at how it twisted and curved with those serrated edges. "This is the nastiest thing I have ever seen."

Hawke laughed, took it from him and staggered for the table. "Imagine what fuckin mess I could do with two." She grabbed her guns and reholstered them before collecting her rifle.

He observed her moving towards the door. The shake was back in her legs.

"We've given the fuckers long enough." There was tiredness in her voice. "Time to get the fuck outta here."

"You do not seem too concerned?"

"Know what that fucker is now. We've got the advantage." Hawke pointed at Grong's body with her dagger before trying again to sheath it. With a low curse, she managed. "That's a fuckin golem."

"Golem?"

"Brain's in a box, in a ship in orbit." Hawke looked at the corridors again. "Fuckin expensive setup." She checked the battery on her rifle. "Need a fuckin map. What is takin Chris so fuckin long?"

"Wait, a map?" Eric shouldered the rifle and dug into his jacket pocket.

The map he had bought from the Sirius trader was still there. He pulled it out and turned it on. It zoomed in on their position in sections. He noted the residential levels as it opened a blank, unmapped area with the indicator looking like it floated in space.

Eric sighed. "Mars, this thing was a waste of money." He raised it to show her. "When I bought it, it had Rebeal tagged as closed. I was told it would update directly from Sirius's network but it never has." He flicked the map off and moved to toss it.

"Give it." Hawke extended a hand and took it. She flicked the casing open and turned it back on. "Yep, connected to Ricki, alright."

"Ricki?"

"Sirius's Controller." Hawke touched the circuit inside with a finger. "Fuckin little arsewipe. He's probably gettin kickbacks to keep areas off the public maps."

Eric watched, fascinated, as small sparks of light flashed across her eyes. In seconds, their commlinks beeped connection.

Chris said, <Wait. That is not... Captain?>

Hawke snorted and Eric laughed. "What's takin you so fuckin long?"

Chris, <Grong has a rotating algorithm. The second we break the sequence, it changes.>

Denthar said, <Grong's got some nice gear. Des?>

Desmond said, <Got the location. We are on our way.>

"We've got some time. I triggered Grong's recall for his hunters. They'll regroup and then we'll fuckin have some fun with them."

Hawke set her rifle against her arm and turned back to Eric. The datastream in her eyes preceded the warning in Eric's commlink. A second channel overrode the main line.

"Wolf?"

Coni said, <Still shutdown.>

Nina growled, looking at her watch. "Ok. You two get the sled and met us at Rebeal. I think Bob's gonna wanna see the end of this clusterfuck."

Chris, <On our way. Need anything?>

"A fuckin whiskey."

Eric chuckled.

She looked at him before adding, "Tell Bob to crack into the rum again too." The line pinged back to the mains.

Denthar, <Hillar, you still breathin?>

Hawke motioned for Eric to answer and to lead the way out of the room.

"I am fine."

He listened for noise before opening the door and peeking into the corridor. More double doors filled the hall ahead of them. A few people wandered through them and the crossroads ahead. In the far distance, Eric saw the harsh light of the main column and could hear the low hum of transports.

"Captain got a blast in the back from Grong's cannon, though," he added.

Hawke made a low growl, causing Eric to look at her. She was glaring at him. He shrugged at her.

Desmond, <Nina?>

"I'm fuckin fine." The voice dripped menace for whoever contradicted her.

"She has had a Medivi... But—"

"Mr fuckin Hillar." She pushed past him and headed out into the corridor.

"You want me to trust, you learn to accept help."

Hawke stopped and turned, looking up at him. She shook her head as they heard laughter from Desmond and Denthar.

Desmond, <Hillar, one thing you will learn about our esteemed Queen of Pirates, she never needs the help.>

Eric raised his eyebrows at her and she rolled her eyes, waiting.

Desmond continued, <At least, even if she does... she will never admit it.>

They continued moving down the corridor towards the main column.

"I honestly don't know which one of you is the bigger fuckin arse," she bit back. "Or, more delusional. I'll ask for help when I fuckin know that person will come through with it."

Desmond, <Our golden-haired leader seems to be trying something new, Dent.>

Denthar, <Next thing we know, she'll stand back and let someone else do something.>

Hawke rubbed at her temple, still glaring at Eric. He grinned back, realising that she was more annoyed at the attention on her than the concern for her injuries.

"Just make sure you have an armour patch ready for me." She shrugged at Eric. "I like this fuckin jacket."

She dropped her hand as they reached the entrance to the main area and pointed at a nearby park space.

Eric saw several families a few metres away, with children playing on the equipment and parents watching.

Hawke ignored them. She sat on a table in the centre of a grassed and treed green space. She rested the rifle on her lap and watched the traffic of the core.

Upon seeing her weapon, several adults rushed to their children and ushered them away into nearby living quarters.

"Is this really the best place?" Eric joined her, leaning against the table as she watched the last of the families disappear through a door. The lock on it blinked green.

"I didn't fuckin choose where Grong put the Safehouse." She stretched back.

Eric winced at her growl.

"Dent, you left yet?"

Denthar, <About to. Why?>

"Bring your transports. Might as well make a few creds out of this."

Eric snorted. "Because you have not pissed Grong off enough yet?"

"Of course fuckin not." She rolled her eyes. "I'm finishin what it fuckin started."

Eric looked at Hawke's face as he asked his next question. "Why are you calling Grong, 'it'?"

She gave him a cold smile. "Same reason I call you, he." She rubbed at her neck and looked at the children's play area. "They call me the ice bitch, not a fuckin arsehole. Respect where it's due."

She lifted her hand and turned her commline off. She kept her eyes on the playground as she spoke. "Something you gotta know, Mr Hillar."

Eric straightened a little but did not speak.

"Kei'll never be on Wolf."

He blinked, went to speak but stopped as she went on.

Hawke's eyes never left the playground. "She doesn't belong to Wolf." Those eyes finally turned to look at him, a genuine half smile on her lips. "Some people make their own path, regardless of what they leave behind."

He turned his own commlink off before speaking. "Why are you telling me this?"

"Crew." Nina shrugged and turned back to the playground. "The long hauls get lonely out here, and I know Martians are poly… Coni doesn't."

Eric chuckled. "Is the feared Captain Hawke giving life advice now?"

"Take what you can out here." She growled and stretched. "I'm not sayin do, I'm not sayin don't but don't dismiss without a fuckin conversation."

"You are giving life advice." Eric snorted. "And you are pretty open about things."

She shrugged. "Realist."

"Point." Eric leaned against the park bench. "So, answer me this: Cinas are a product of evolution across the subs, not a distinct one themselves. You, however, strike me as something different again. Where are you really from?"

"Wolf."

Eric laughed. "Captain?"

"Wolf's my home. She always fuckin will be." She grunted and she rested her arms and rifle on her knees.

"So… That mess you mentioned leaving behind." Eric kept his eyes ahead of them but watched for her reaction in the corner of his vision. "Was it called Jake?"

She swung her head sharply to stare at him. Her expression was completely unreadable.

"Forget I asked."

"No." Her eyes narrowed. After a long exhale she turned from him. Her shoulders dropping as she relaxed. "Didn't leave any fuckin mess behind that was called Jake, Mr Hillar."

Eric lapsed into silence, replaying their conversation through his thoughts. A small smile edged his lips when he thought about her words and the care it implied.

After some time, Eric looked up as several transports, about the same size as the one on Werewolf, landed near them, completely ignoring the landing pads near the core.

The airlocks opened and several people jumped out. Hawke put her hand on Eric's shoulder as he brought his rifle around to aim. She inclined her head and dropped her hand after he relaxed.

"Eric?" Kei broke from the first group and reached them at a flat run.

He caught her as she jumped into his arms, her long air swinging around them. He paused, feeling the weapons across her chest. He looked down. She had adorned the inviting skin-tight dress with a shoulder strap of knives and a hip holster, the handgun anchored it into place.

"Are you ok?" She smiled when Eric nodded.

"You?" He breathed when she inclined her head and pouted.

"I am fine." Kei did not look away from Eric. She smiled. "Left enough of them bloody for easy identification later. Rebeal does not like it when people try to take services for free from their staff."

"And you wonder why I'd rather fuckin shoot them." Hawke growled and turned to watch Denthar and another man heading towards them.

Black-skinned with bright green hair, the man with Denthar looked the part of a pirate with a bottle of alcohol in one hand and a large semi-automatic in the other. Violet eyes with laughter lines became visible as he got closer.

Denthar was holding a small box that Eric recognised as an armour field repair kit.

"Show the crews the safehouse," Hawke told Eric as she watched the two men approach. "Give me a few minutes here."

Eric nodded.

"Kei?" Eric asked her quietly.

She waved at the others to follow. She looked back at him and smiled. "Later. Orders first."

Eric glanced at the patch on Hawke's jacket. She had applied it to the hole while he showed Denthar and Desmond's crews the holding cell and the rooms of equipment. He noted the shine of new metal against the blackened leather, as they stepped onto the familiar grillwork in front of Rebeal. Denthar and Desmond stood behind them with some of their crew members.

Hawke stopped, looking at the front of Rebeal's black wall.

"How do you want to play this, Nina?" Denthar asked.

Eric turned to see that the captains had moved a little closer to Hawke and him.

She smiled darkly at Eric, then turned to look at the pair. "Grong's goin for our bounties." She adjusted her jacket. "And won't stop until it's convinced the prize isn't fuckin worth it."

She looked up at Eric. "Ready to make a mess, Mr Hillar?"

"Captain." Eric nodded.

"We'll flush them. Des, Dent... ready for some huntin?"

"Always, my golden-haired, blood-soaked siren." Desmond motioned to his crew and disappeared into the corridors around Rebeal.

Denthar and Hawke looked at each other.

"Well... he's right about one thing," Denthar inclined his head and moved in the other direction, continuing into his commlink, <you love to get bloody.>

"Maybe I can fuckin sing, Dent. Ever fuckin thought of that?" Hawke snorted as they heard multiple laughter through the comms.

Denthar, <That would be worth somethin to hear.>

"Chris?"

Chris said, <Business as normal in here, Captain.>

Coni said, <Left Angel with a pile of those circuits to play with. We have about an hour before he looks for us.>

"This won't take long." She looked at Eric. "Remember what you said in Rebeal that standard we met? About pointin guns in people's faces?"

Eric's eyes narrowed when she laughed coldly.

"Now's the time to show your fuckin intentions."

"You heard that?"

She answered him with that cruel twist at the edge of her mouth.

Eric shook his head, and they stepped towards the door. The green paint glowed slightly off the picture of the Terran hand flipping them the bird.

"Kei is right. You are as bloodthirsty as they come."

"Gotta enjoy what you do, Mr Hillar, or what's the fuckin point of it all?" Sharp teeth flashed in the green light.

They entered the bar together. Once inside, Eric had that instant feeling of being watched. The normal hum of the bar dulled.

Chris, ::No sign of Grong, but he has a few of his hunters monitoring the place. Second mezzanine.:: The sound of the Kat's voice was metallic and toneless.

Eric narrowed his eyes. Chris was not using his speaker to transmit the words. His commlink was generating them from commands the cyborg had sent over the connection digitally.

Chris, ::Watch your back, Captain.::

The dark smile that spread across Hawke's face was enough to make several of those at the bar pale and move quickly away.

Eric cleared his throat to hide the amusement.

"Grong's armour is pretty much unbreachable." Hawke leaned against the bar and motioned to Bob.

The Custurian looked at Eric and seemed to smile, the tentacles turning up on the sides of his mouth.

"Best bet is to fire down the cannon's mouth."

"Cause a misfire?" Eric watched the room while Bob poured them drinks. "Not an easy target. And it must activate the cannon to begin with."

Hawke lifted her glass to her lips and sculled it as Eric turned back to pick up his own drink. Bob watched them.

"Fried its body, cleaned out its safehouse and huntin its people. Don't worry, it'll activa—" She stopped as the bar went deathly quiet. The sound of a large energy weapon powering up was loud in comparison. She put the tumbler down before turning.

Eric placed his glass under the rim of the bar, protecting it.

Bob looked at Eric's hand, then his face and nodded.

Grong had entered the space from behind them. The main doors of Rebeal shut as Eric focused on the cyborg. It stopped only a few metres from them. The body was the same, only this time, the waves and swirls were not blue, but a deep mustard colour. It pointed the cannon at them and powered up, green lights blinking.

Eric felt the instant kick in his gut to run, to survive, then Hawke moved in front of him.

"I do not make the same mistake twice." Grong's metallic voice almost echoed in the silence. "I should just kill you."

"Maybe." The ponytail dropped to the side as she studied the cyborg's new body.

Eric raised his rifle, aiming over her head at Grong. Seeing Hawke face down a walking, armoured tank, that was at least a metre taller than her, was not something he expected when stepping off Werewolf several hours earlier.

"But where's the fuckin fun in that?"

Grong seemed to consider her words for a moment, then Eric saw something he had never expected to in a cyborg... fear. The cannon pointed at her shook slightly, as if being forced to stay. Its limbs pulled back a little as the mechanics of its eyes dilated. The weapon was powered, but Grong had not triggered the firing sequence.

The commlink in Eric's ear pinged, then trilled a sequence he had never heard before.

Hawke's shoulders dropped back and she straightened. In her ear was a flood of colour from her commlink indicator.

Angel said, <I want Coolios.>

"See. Fuckin useful." There was a dark amusement in her tone.

The cannon quivered, lowering a little as data streamed across Grong's eyes.

"Wolf." Hawke's command rang through the bar. Lights flickered, datascreens turned to static.

Eric looked up at the lights of the bar, his commlink doing that strange trill again. He refocused on Grong, understanding now the cyborg's words were meaningless. Hawke and Grong were fighting some data war in Sirius's network. A battle of wills and code.

Grong's arm straightened again. "I know what you are."

"That just makes the game more fuckin fun."

Eric blinked as Hawke took a few steps forward, the hole of the cannon touching her chest.

"Don't ever fuckin forget, Grong... I've been in your head."

Something triggered in Grong's system and its body powered down.

Hawke dodged off to the side, sprinting for the mezzanines.

Hawke said, <Got about two minutes before the fucker resets.>

Eric looked above and saw a man aiming his rifle at Hawke. Eric aimed and fired, moving towards the cover of the bar edge. Seconds later, he dodged forward, away from the splattering of fire aimed from the top level.

Chris and Coni moved out of the shadows at the far end of the bar. Chris covered his sister with a rifle as she slipped past him, pulling his handgun out of the hip holster. The pair turned and fired, covering each other's back.

Hawke jumped onto a table, then caught the rail of the second level with a hand and somersaulted over it into the crowd.

Eric smiled at the surprised shouts and the pained screams coming from the area she had landed.

From the back of the room, Denthar materialised out of the shadows, his gun aimed.

Eric felt a bullet skim his shoulder. Turning in the direction it came from, he fired, taking out a woman. Her cybernetic eyes froze as they fried from the energy shot.

Chris said, <Werewolf cannot stop the connection for long.>

Hawke, <Long enough.>

From the third level, several people jumped over the rails, trying to escape the fight, and landed on the floor near Eric. They groaned as they hit the surface hard. Somersaulting through the air, Hawke followed them, landing in a crouch.

Blood covered her face and hair, along with the hand holding her dagger. The dark blade dripped thick crimson liquid onto the grillwork. The room filled with the acrid smell of energy bullets and the metallic stench of blood.

The sound of gears powering up near Eric made him turn. He watched Grong's frame shake, their systems rebooting. The lights in its body and the cannon flickered on, then turned solid.

Hawke looked up from her landing, eyes bright as she fixed them on the cyborg.

Eric saw the datastream speeding across her eyes.

"Hillar." Grong ignored the sounds of the fight around them and focused on him. "Help me take her down."

Eric aimed his rifle at Grong, moving slowly to get out from between the cyborg and the bar. The cyborg's cannon followed his movement. Eric breathed slowly, forcing himself to focus, waiting for the moment where he could trigger a misfire.

"Do it and I will let you go free."

"Free?"

"No hunters, no hiding." Several antennas on Grong's back lifted out of their casing and swivelled, trying to get a lock on some signal. "I can make it so you never have to run again."

Eric felt the unsaid like a hammer in his guts. He looked back at Hawke, the rifle heavy in his hands. Everything he knew of the UTC told him they would do anything to have her back or dead.

"You saw what she did to me. You know what she truly is. The deal you could make with the UTC... You could have whatever you want."

Eric thought of his Josie.

"Decide, Hillar." Grong said.

Hawke looked at him, blood sliding down her cheek and neck. She turned her back to them and made her way through the crowd, gun firing as she slashed with the blade in her other hand.

"Your freedom for hers."

The image of Grong's freeze came into his mind. The cyborg's words seemed strange for the reputation it had for never letting a target go. It had taken Hawke down, but was now asking for help? The realisation was a light turning on in Eric's mind: she had hacked Grong. It could not fight or even shoot at her.

Grong was attempting to use him to divide and win. All that waited for him was a UTC cell and a trip to a penal planet. Anger bubbled at the lies, the play, the UTC-style manipulation. He thought of Hawke and how she had trusted him enough to turn her back and leave him to deal with the cyborg.

"Not much of a choice, Grong."

Light built up in the cannon's barrel.

Eric raised his rifle, aimed and squeezed the trigger. The energy bullet hit its mark. The metal of the cannon peeled back as the explosion shattered Grong from the inside.

He tried to move out of the way, but the blast was too fast, too intense. Heat burned at his skin.

A shadow rolled over Eric. Hawke lunged in front of him, her gun and knife crossed over, protecting her face.

Energy roared as it crashed across them. The air burned Eric's lungs, followed by a tingling sensation, as more energy washed over him like a wave.

The force of the impact pushed them backwards, hurling them through the front wall, then onto the grillwork. Hawke fell back onto him, sending crushing pain across his chest as she landed.

Hawke rolled and growled, staggering to her knees. Her gun fizzled and sparked. She used the barrel tip on the grillwork to steady herself.

Eric coughed. His lungs continued to burn from the heat and his ribs ached from the impact. He rolled to his side and struggled onto his elbow before stopping. His vision blurred, stomach twisted.

She turned towards him, her eyes narrowing.

"Stay down." She contradicted her words by trying to stand up and failing. "Now that was a fuckin move. Next time you cover my back, keep your arse outta the kill range."

"Captain." Eric lay back down, smiling, as he acknowledged the order, the comment, and the compliment. There was a dull thump in his temple.

He lifted his hand to the side of his skull and winced at the pain upon touch. His fingers came away wet. He looked at the blood smeared across them. "Think we are done with this pissing contest yet?"

"Two bodies in as many fuckin hours. I think it got the fuckin hint, Eric."

He groaned, dropping his hand to his chest. "First names now?"

"Prefer Captain." She settled back on her legs. Raising the gun to look at it. "But, if you fuckin must, it's Hawke." Her tone was hard, but there was a slight smile. "You've got a few more raids before you've earned that fuckin right."

"Ok, Captain. Only when we are in the shit, then." Eric laughed and Hawke snorted. He then winced as pain shot across the back of his skull. "Now what?"

She tossed the sparking gun onto the grillwork and raised her head. After another failed attempt to stand, she sat on her knees.

"A fuckin drink."

Eric laughed, then groaned again. He could see Coni running towards them.

Hawke ran her hand over her head and down her ponytail as he heard her chuckle.

Plastic sheets boarded up the front wall of Rebeal. Workers cleaned the broken shards out of the framing.

Eric leaned back, settling the glass of rum on his thigh. Next to him, Kei was checking a throwing blade she was holding, her tail slithering around his other leg. He winced watching the workers, remembering the pain from the shards of glass-like material that Coni had dug out from the back of his head.

"Seriously, kid, you're gonna get heartburn." Denthar pointed a finger at Angel from his spot on the other side of the table. He watched the boy shove fistfuls of Coolios chips into his mouth.

From Angel's seat on Hawke's lap, he considered Denthar's words for a minute.

"You're right." He grabbed the burger that was slowly sliding down the steaming pile of chips. "Meat first."

Angel opened the burger, pulled the veg out and tossed them to the edge of the chip wrapping before cramming the bun back down and biting into it with relish.

Denthar stared at him open-mouthed before Desmond whacked the captain on the shoulder, laughing hard.

"No denying the kid has been around her too long, that's for sure, Jake."

Hawke raised her eyebrows, lifting a tumbler to her lips.

Between Eric and her, the Kats watched the crowd around Rebeal. Their attention was on someone at the bar. Coni's ears twitched as Chris drank an iced coffee. Eric wondered how it did not freeze his mechanics, but Chris appeared to be enjoying it.

Ana was sitting with Denthar, leaning against him as she checked her handgun.

Desmond stretched, leaning back in his chair. He glanced at what had the Kats so fixated.

"Did Grong finally get the datastream?" Desmond draped an arm over the back of his chair and looked at the cyborg, the mustard shoulders high above anyone else at the bar.

"Would want to hope so." Denthar smiled and inclined his glass towards Nina. "He had to buy both his bodies back from the junk dealer. They would not have been cheap. Not after pissin the harbourmaster off."

"It learned that fuckin lesson. So, we let it continue the game." Hawke gave him a twisted smile in return. "But it'll have to learn a new one if it ain't fuckin careful who it associates with." She snorted as they all turned to look at the bar.

"One standard, you gotta explain the game you're playin, Nina." Denthar muttered.

She inclined her head at him but did not speak.

The man talking to Grong looked nondescript. His short brown hair was neat and the suit he wore was a plain, black cloth that screamed money in its simplicity.

Eric's shoulders tightened as he recognised the style and cut of the clothes.

"Who is that?" Kei leaned on the table, following Eric's gaze.

"That is the new FIS agent." Desmond smiled.

They noticed the man turn to look in their general direction.

"Cockroach." Hawke growled as she drank.

Eric glanced at her. She watched the bar intently, but there was a small smile that contradicted the low snarl he heard.

"I heard his name was Quinten Brown. Used to be some big shot on an Alati team. Who knows what mess he got into to be sent out here." Desmond added.

"I thought Paul was the new FIS?" Ana glanced under the mezzanines, towards the stairs.

"After what Varsely pulled at that mining colony, I'd expect the UTC wants a few more eyes out here that know Alatis." Denthar shrugged at the thought. "They're pushin, Nina."

"We'll just have to fly further." She put her tumbler down and watched Quinten turn to Grong, say something, then motion to one of Bob's wives.

Eric shared a smile with Kei as the FIS approached the table, a tumbler of whiskey in hand. Ignoring the group, he stopped in front of Hawke and slid the glass to her.

She caught it before it slipped off the table. Her eyebrows raised as she lifted it, her gaze never leaving him.

"Captain Hawke." Quinten inclined his head, smiling slightly. "Figured payin my respects was better than avoidin potential… problems later."

"Warn Paul that hidin out in the fuckin shadows is not the way to stay off my fuckin radar."

"You know about him? No subtlety to the man at all." Quinten sighed and looked around the table. "Captains Denthar and Rowe." He nodded at them, then turned to Eric. "Eric Hillar. Now that's a report I'll enjoy filin later. You'll have to tell me one rotation about how you collapsed those caverns in Olympus Mons."

Eric tensed.

"I always wonder at the engineerin of those sorts of explosions. I find it fascinatin how you can almost direct their energy."

Eric saw Hawke tense, but she kept her gaze on the FIS.

Quinten turned back to her and looked at the boy.

Eric shifted, ready to reach for his gun.

The FIS agent paled, his throat shifting as he swallowed.

Eric watched Hawke while Quinten stared. She did not move and purely stared back. Eric breathed, wondering what had the FIS rattled. Did he recognise Hawke? Know what she was? Know what the boy was?

"I'm here for the Alatis." He seemed to recover. "Any information on their movements that you find in your travels will be paid for rather well, Captain." He smiled. "Captain Hawke… I like the ring of that."

Quinten inclined his head again and turned, walking out the main entrance. The door with the painted stylised Terran hand slid shut behind him.

"Different." Denthar watched the door well after Quinten left.

"Cockroach." Nina repeated. "Knows how to fuckin survive."

Eric lowered his hand from his gun.

"So, what's next for you, Des?" Denthar turned away from her, deliberately ignoring the frosty smile.

"Got a line on some supplies that might make a good profit with the drifters."

"Watch your back." Chris's ears turned, following the sounds of movement behind him. "Been hearing that some of them are trading with Fleet—trading bounties they find for supplies."

Coni turned her back to the table. Her tail swung slowly in the air as she leaned on her chair so she could people-watch those in the bar.

"You, Jake?" Desmond waved the concern away.

"Got some merchant convoys that're a little cargo heavy."

"Hawke?" Desmond turned to her.

"I know a trader who needs to be fuckin reminded not to put private contracts out on me."

"Captain..." Coni purred nervously.

"Our Rim, Con." Hawke's tone was metal. "He brought Alati soldiers into our fuckin Rim."

Coni's ears twisted. "I just do not want to find a new captain."

Denthar laughed, sharing a look with Hawke. "They'll catch us all one-rotation, Coni."

Hawke inclined her head at the comment.

"Enjoy torturin the arsehole." Denthar stood up and finished his beer, placing the glass on the table. He motioned to Kei. "Charger should be loaded by now."

"Coming, Captain." Kei stroked Eric's arm and stood, leaving pins and needles in her hand's wake. She smiled at Eric, nodded to the others, and followed Denthar out of the bar.

"Varsely, Captain?" Coni's ears pinned, her tail tucked between her legs.

"You're the one that wants fuckin upgrades in Medibay."

Eric smiled as Coni turned, looked at Hawke, then resumed her people watching.

"You sure you want to stay on Wolf, Hillar? She can get grumpy." Desmond laughed, stretching.

Eric inclined his head to Hawke as she rolled her eyes at Desmond.

"Someone needs to have her back." Eric put his rum down and turned to look at Angel. "And, convince her and the kid to eat greens eventually." He smiled while the others laughed.

Hawke looked at the ceiling and inhaled deeply.

ACKNOWLEDGEMENTS

THIS BOOK WAS ONLY POSSIBLE WITH
THE HELP OF :

MY WORKSHOP CREW, WHO KNOW
THE UNIVERSE OF TIDE BETTER THAN I
DO.

THE CHAOS CORNER AND ITS
COMMUNITY ON YOUTUBE, WHO
HELPED ME FIND MY VOICE AGAIN.

ABOUT THE AUTHOR

Renee lives with her husband and four children (two furred and two humanoid) in Australia.

After years of procrastination and writing as an off-on hobby, she finally took it seriously during maternity leave and digitally dusted off an old manuscript and reworked her science fiction series, *Tide of the Stars*. *Descent* is the first book based in that universe.

When she isn't writing or wallowing in the chaos of family life, Renee can be found on YouTube as Fictional Crafts documenting her writing, reading and crafty journey.

To get the news first on any of Renee's upcoming releases, visit **www.rahowes.com** and sign up to the email list.